THAILAND TRIANGLE

BOOK TWO

JD WILLIAMS

SWEETSPIRE LITERATURE
MANAGEMENT

WOULD LIKE TO THANK MY WIFE
DIANA MY BEST FRIEND.

ALSO BY J.D. WILLIAMS

IN PURSUIT OF THE INNOCENT COME
TO BED WITH MOTHER

I WOULDN'T CHANGE A THING "A TRILOGY
OF CRIME" "WHERE IS HENRY?"

FULL CIRCLE "SCI FI SERIES"

THE PILGRIMS OF GLIESE THE END GAME

DESTRUCTION OF THE ORION NEBULA

LIST OF CHARACTERS;

JACK MORRISON – DETECTIVE

HENRY - SHAPESHIFTER, CRIMINAL

CARL - CRIMINAL, MURDERER

GEORGE WILSON - HEAD OF CIA IN THAILAND

MARJORIE SWIFT - CIA AGENT

SARA - MARJORIE'S DAUGHTER

SUSAN ALCOTT - SARA'S GUARDIAN

A-WUT - THAILAND DOUBLE AGENT

HOM - CALL GIRL

DEREK WATSEN - RICH, MONEY LAUNDERING FOR MOB

JOHNNY - CIA AGENT

SAM - FEMALE AGENT UNDERCOVER

BIG CHARLEY - MOB BOSS

TWO FINGERS - MADE MAN

PHYLLIS - CASINO HOST

DOMINIC MARETTO – LAWYER

JEFFERSONS - MURDERED COUPLE

Chapter One

Detective Morrison is relaxing having a Bourbon neat, thinking,"This is the life, after I cracked the case in Los Angeles they decided to send me to Thailand to track down Henry and Carl. Those two have been spotted dealing drugs and illegal prostitution." He sat back buckling his seat belt as the plane coasted to a landing at don Mueang International Airport, Thailand.

He deplaned and waited at the entrance of the terminal for his meeting with George Wilson a CIA Agent, he scanned the crowded promenade for his contact. The place was alive with Chinese, Indians and foreign Tourists thinking,"What a melange of humanity, this part of the world was growing by leaps and bounds." Morrison set his briefcase on the seat next to him, then a porter ran over and picked it up explaining, "Please sir follow me to limousine, hurry, hurry!"

"Who in the hell are you? get your scrubby hands off of my briefcase." Morrison hollered,"Please mister my name A-wut my boss George Wilson ask me take you to Riva Surya Bangkok Hotel he say tell you he will meet you there." Morrison bowed,"Sorry what did you say your name was again?" My name A-Wut I Mr.Wilson interpreter,"he answered.

"Ok, A-Wut lets get on the road George is waiting." When they exited the airport the heat engulfed Morrison, "Jesus, I am going to have to shed this suit before I die, this heat is a killer." He removed his jacket, tie and dress shirt, tapped A-Wut on the shoulder,"Please, wait here a couple of minutes." Morrison entered a shop facing the street bought the brightest shirt in the store, when the clerk gave him the price he bowed politely and answered with a thank you in Thai. Put the shirt on and left the store,"Ok A-Wat let's roll on to the hotel."

It was a twenty minute drive to the hotel, as soon as the limousine pulled to the curb A-Wat opened the door for Morrison, and bowed,"Please boss you don't have to sign in just go to room 326 Mr. Wilson waiting for you. I will take care of your luggage and bring it to your room."

Morrison walked through the hotel lobby taking in the sights, to his left he spots a couple of call girls sitting on one of the couches giving him the eye, she was a slender girl with long silky black hair and misty eyes giving him a smile. She is maybe eighteen years old, she points to herself then back to him, he smiles back and is about to shake his head no, but instead leans over to his guide whispers,"Have the pretty one with the long hair come to my room in a couple of hours, do you know her name?"A-Wat answers,"Her name Hom it means fragrant in Thai." Morrison asks,"How did she get such a pleasant name, or is that her working name?"

"No, that her birth name, she's my sister we work as a team so we can pay our rent and eat." Morrison continues,"Where are your parents, do they live with you or are they deceased?" A-Wat,"We live with our parents they are very ill, I also have a younger sister and brother."As they are conversing the elevator door opens they both enter Morrison is silent, thinking to himself,"I can use these two to guide me through the back alleys and enlighten me to the workings of the underworld in Bangkok. There is quite a bit of trafficking in drugs, prostitution, and bribery, that's why it's known as the Thailand Triangle." The elevator stops at the third floor and they disembark, he follows A-Wat to the suite where his CIA contact is waiting. Before they can knock George Wilson opens the door,"Welcome to my world Morrison come in have a drink, relax, nice shirt you fit right in as a tourist." The two men sat down and spent a few minutes gauging each others strengths and weaknesses, finally George broke the silence he was a former seal with the rank of Colonel stood six foot three, blond hair, steely blue eyes and muscles all the way to his toes. He had a propensity for the beautiful Thai women and they definitely enjoyed his company. The only foreigner that enjoyed the girls at some of the clubs at no charge. George,"Morrison I personally asked for you to be the liaison between the CIA and Law Enforcement in the States, we have a real problem in Thailand and Cambodia, Carl and Harry are into gun running, drugs, prostitution, you name it. There are rumors they are buying weapons from China and Russia and selling the weapons to insurgents in the southern part of Thailand. As you know Thailand has a problem with the Muslims down south they are attempting to force the government to give them autonomy.Carl,"Supplying them with weapons is giving the Thai Government a royal headache. The Thai's have asked us to give them a hand to find those two assholes and take them back to the states."George continued to brief Morrison on what was known about Harry and Carl,"We have a algorithm that monitors the internet, there has been a rash of brutal attacks on prostitutes that are a mirror image of those committed in the States.The Thai Government ignored our warnings until the attacks were perpetrated on foreign tourists,"Then all hell broke loose, the Tourists stayed away and the revenue plunged they came to the Embassy looking for help. You are the only one who knows what this Henry actually looks like. He appeals to women on the internet with a sob story that makes them feel sorry for him. As you know he sets up a clandestine meeting drugs the woman rapes, beats her and when she is asked for a description it is never the same." Morrison sits listening and speaks,"I will start by interviewing all the madams at the clubs to see if we can place Harry, if you don't mind I would like to have the services of A-Wat and Hom his sister as interpreters when I visit the clubs." Morrison, "What exactly do you want from me?" George,"There will be a three prong assault, we have in-beds in the south monitoring the radical group, we need you to track down Harry and Carl, the Thai Secret Service has eyes on the drug traffic this suite will be the focal point for all operations. Our biggest problem is stopping the drug trade they are using the money from the sale of drugs to purchase weapons from the Russians and Chinese then sell them to the insurgents."

Chapter Two

Morrison turns around and speaks to A-Wat,"Can you call your sister have her and you come to my room in about an hour that will give me time to clean up, I'll need your help questioning the club owners to see what information we can glean about Henry's whereabouts."After the briefing Morrison walked to his room unlocked the door, dropped his coat on the couch and started to undress, leaving his clothes on the tile floor. He walked nude into the bathroom stepped into the shower, turned on the cold water, reaching in letting the water run through his fingers. Stepped into the shower in feeling the water cause his blood to flow energizing his tall frame, after a few minutes when he was awakened turned on the hot water, stood there till he felt his body relax and soaped his lean male torso, rinsed off.In his younger years he had completed an eight year tour as an Airborne Ranger, and relished the mental and physical demands placed on his mind and body, now at forty six still made the grade. After his shower he slipped into a pair of walking shorts and sandals, pulled a tight fitting shirt over his head admiring what he saw in the full length mirror in the bathroom. He said to no one in particular,"I still have it, kick ass bad, I will try some martial arts training."He sat on the couch thinking,"I left my ex-wife and daughter back in the states without saying goodby, maybe she was right I live for the job first, everyone else comes last. I hope her next husband is a forty hour a week bleep." There was a knock on the door, he walked to the peep hole it was Hom such a lovely child about his daughters age. Opening the door motioned her into the room. Hom asked,"What you want me to do for you? I do anything for a hundred American dollars for fifty more I stay all day, my brother say you good pay." Morrison holds up his hands,"Hold on there Hom, I told your brother I wanted to talk, why don't you just take your little butt over to the table sit down so we can talk." She looked downcast,"You no like me?I can do anything you want I will please you I promise." Morrison,"Yes, I like you, but I need you and your brother to act as my interpreters I didn't ask you up here for sex, I am looking for very bad men I will pay you and your brother what ever you think is fair." There is a knock on the door. Morrison,"Come on in, we have been waiting for you A-Wat why don't you and your sister sit with me at the table? I have pictures I would like you to look at and see if you recognize any one."They walk to the table Morrison places pictures of Henry and Carl for them to identify,"Have you seen either of these men in the last week?"

A-Wat shakes his head,"No I don't recognize them." Hom,"This one looks familiar different hair and facial features he start fight in Cockatoo Club, we nickname him Ling because he move like monkey when he angry. He was in club last Wednesday. Club in Soi Cowboy neighborhood of Bangkok it really shaking at night." Morrison thinks to himself,"Sounds like we have a good start, maybe this is Henry's favorite hangout, alright why don't we meet at the Cockatoo Club at eight tonight and I'll question the Madame,"Hopefully she can shed some light on this mans whereabouts or some of his habits. Please keep this to yourselves he is extremely dangerous,I don't want anyone hurt." A-wat and Hom agreed to the time and place when they left,"Morrison walked down the hall and knocked on Charley's door,"Morrison come in, come in." George was sitting at the computer, looking up asked,"What can I do for you,Morrison?" "I am meeting with your interpreter A-Wat and his sister at eight tonight, to make the rounds at the Soi Cowboy area, maybe I can get a handle on Henry? Hom recognizes him as a client at the club. Is it Ok, if I borrow your boy?" Charley,"Be my guest, I'm going south for a week or so, there's rumors of a weapons sale in the near future, the Thai Government is lending me a squad of their special forces for backup. Keep me appraised of your operation, call me on my encrypted phone every night at twelve."Morrison answered,"I have your back my friend, have no fear."Morrison was deep into studying a map of the Bangkok hot spots when his phone rang, "Hello, who is this?" Hotel Clerk,"This is the desk Mr.Morrison your taxi is waiting."

"All right will be down shortly." Morrison picks up his ankle gun and automatic pistol, makes sure they are loaded, straps on the ankle gun adjusts his shoulder holster, places his automatic and is ready to take on the night. He activates the hall camera and places a silk thread across the threshold, checks his app to make sure the cameras in the apartment are working, smiles contentedly takes the elevator to the lobby. Walking across the hotel lobby notices a couple of men lounging against the bar, stops to pick up a local paper so he can get a better look, sure as hell they have been following him they were at the airport, look Russian. As a matter a fact really burly Russians they could be a problem. He pulls out his phone and takes their picture sends it to the CIA to see if they can identify them with a note,"I am being following are they ours or someone I should be wary of?"

CHAPTER THREE

Morrison enters the cab and sits in the back, the cabbie asks,"Where to boss?"."Take me to the Soi Cowboy neighborhood and drop me off at the Cockatoo Club,I need some action" he quips.The cabbie laughs,"You get action at Soy Cowboy mister, all kinds of action." The ride takes twenty minutes Morrison pays for the ride steps out onto the sidewalk. He is immediately surrounded by Thai"B"girls, "Mister you buy me drink, you want massage?" he waves them off,"Sorry girls already have a date."Spots A-Wat standing at the entrance, puts his finger to his lips and walks right past him whispering,"Meet me inside." Once inside he turns and looks down the street to make sure he hasn't been tailed. Sure as shit there across the street were the two Russian apes. The cab driver probably gave them my location."Alright guys lets find the Madam and see if she can enlighten us."They walked up the stairs and at the landing was an office, A-Wat asks,"Can we see Madam please?" They stand in the hall for a few minutes and the door opens,"Please come in she will see you now." Sitting behind a large desk sat a woman in her late forties black hair, large green colored eyes, looked younger than her actual age. "How may I help you Lieutenant Morrison? I understand you are looking for "Harry the Ling." A slight smile crossed her lips. Morrison wondered,"How in the hell did she know what my name is? This entire scenario is getting out of hand."

"May I ask, how did you know who I was looking for? There seems to be an extreme amount of interest in our investigation. Outside of the club there is a couple of Russian goons shadowing me. Maybe you can clue me in."

The Madam raises from her chair walking around the desk and stands in front of Morrison,"The Thai Government has asked me to inform you that they will supply you and George with all the information necessary to apprehend and remove Henry and Carl from the country. As to the Russians they are involved with illegal prostitution they are bringing in Uzbek young women and forcing them into sexual slavery, plus gun running. Harry and Carl are somehow involved in this entire enterprise."

Morrison asks,"When was the last time you saw Henry? he is always changing his looks a chameleon can't even keep up with him. He and Carl escaped from the States and landed in Thailand we know Carl is working out of Cambodia. The United States doesn't have an extradition treaty with Cambodia so we can't legally touch him and if Harry crosses the border he'll be home free and we will be shit out of luck." The Madam looks at Morrison," Last time he was here was two weeks ago, he had changed his skin color and appeared to be Indian, only when he started to beat one of my girls did I realize who he was. I had banned him from my establishment about a month ago, he was high on drugs and paid an extra 6,000 Baht for the use of one of my rooms.

Apparently he was so high he didn't realize that his companions were Girlie Boys. So when they started to have their three way sex tryst he was confronted with the fact that he was having sex with two men. Harry went berserker he grabbed the testicles of the Girlie boy on top and literally threw him through my second floor window, just by luck a canvass overhang broke his fall, I am afraid he won't be using his tools anytime soon. The second Girlie Boy he started to beat with his fists when my bodyguards broke down the door. Harry picked up the second poor soul and threw him at the bodyguards, while they were entangled Henry escaped out the window and disappeared into the night. I haven't seen or heard of him since."

Morrison just whistled,"I knew Harry was one crazy son of a bitch, but that takes the cake, both he and Carl have to slake their feelings of rage by beating or raping women.

If I know those two they will show up in the near future looking for someone to prey on."

The Madam spoke again,"I will keep you appraised of any sightings of Americans we want them as bad as your country. As I said they are into every vice known to man, the main problem is they have unlimited funds, so anyone with a price can be bought." Morrison,"I guess we have all we can use at the moment. Oh by the way do you have any idea where this creep may be hiding out?"

"The Thai Police are searching for him as we speak."

Morrison turned to A-Wat and Hom lets go,"Maybe he is plying his trade at the Nana Plaza we should try there next?" They exited the club and were face to face with the two Russian bulls.They were as broad as they were tall both of the Russians had white close cropped hair, blue eyes, bull necks the one standing face to face with Morrison had an iron bar that he bent in two,"You Americans should go home before I bend you like the piece of shit you are. Your friends need to be careful who they deal with, they could get hurt real bad, Oh by the way Henry says HI, Lieutenant Morrison!"

About that time a Police Van pulls alongside the Russians six police exit the van, cross the street truncheons at the ready. The bulls stop talking, turning walk down the street,The sergeant in charge calls to them,"You two what is your business here, if I see you making aggressive movements toward our guest I will slap your asses in jail."

They turn and grunt but keep walking down the street. "Sorry Lieutenant we were held up in traffic, I have no idea what your investigation entails but the entire city is buzzing, everyone knows Henry he is a real piece of work, the word from the Police Chief is to protect you at all cost.Be safe here is my phone number, if you are in danger you can call me day or night." The Thai Police Sergeant turns, returns to the Police Van he waves to his driver to pull away. Morrison,"They want everyone in Bangkok to know what is going on hoping Henry will try to leave the country and get himself arrested trying to cross into Cambodia."

Chapter Four

Henry could feel his mind going into a spiral, down, down made him feel as if he would throw up, he was having blinding headaches, the more drugs he consumed instead of making him feel better he felt worse."What in the hell is the matter with me, I haven't been able to vent my feelings of rage. The damned Police are all over the city, my informant said my picture is plastered in every Club and Whore House in Bangkok. The word on the street is tourists are definitely out of bounds, the country cannot survive without foreign money and they have pegged old Henry as the attacker of the young British woman so my name is shit.

I'll have to move the operation to another town, Carl is going to be pissed, we spent six months setting this up to funnel drugs to Europe and the States, weapons to the Insurgents in the south of Thailand. Now I have to relocate to keep from blowing the entire operation."

Henry opened a map of the area and Sukhumvit stared back at him, of course the area was full of British expats.

"I'll bet quite a few of them would like to make a few bucks carrying drugs.They travel back and forth between England, Australia, Canada it is just a few hours to Cambodia on Route 3, I could meet Carl once a week drop off the cash and do a pick up. Maybe the local cops are doing me a favor." A smile crossed his face,"He was thinking I need a disguise what would keep the authorities guessing? I know what, I will disguise myself as an old lady."

Picking up a magazine laying on the coffee table there was a story about older Thai women. Flipping through the magazine there were pictures of women of prominence in their sixties and seventies. As he slowly turned the pages saw what he was looking, for there she was,"I can scan her face into my "3-D Printer" by this time tomorrow I will have a new face, have to hide the length of my arms, Ah yes! wear a dress and walk with a cane, burnish my exposed skin a light brown, presto I blend in.This disguise will allow me to cross the border into Cambodia when I make my meet with Carl. Henry opens his phone book and looks up the names of his runners, finally he finds the name he's looking for, Charn Chai, always looking to make a fast buck and doesn't care what time of day it is. He dialed his cell phone and sent him a text,"Call me immediately if you want to make some money, Henry."

He pours himself a beer and relaxes on the couch waiting for a reply. Fifteen minutes later his phone lights up with a text,"What you want boss I am with a lady, if you know what I mean." Henry answers,"Meet me at midnight at our usual place bring the truck."He had heard through the grapevine that Morrison was in Bangkok looking for him, "That prick is worse than a pimple on my ass, I will have to put a price on his head. He is in my territory, now I'll screw him up royally, Charn will know someone he can set me up with. A contract killer or maybe one of our Chinese contacts could do the job, I'll talk to Carl tonight to see how much he wants to spend. He has no love for Morrison or Marjorie Swift. As a matter a fact he would love to see them both dead, hell Marjorie almost killed him and Morrison is worse than a blood hound."

Charn met him at the rendezvous exactly at midnight he was driving an old Ford truck it had a half a million miles on it. Harry stayed in the shadows making sure Charn had not been followed, waited for a few minutes after the truck came to a complete stop to expose himself.

Henry,"Ok Charn lets load up when we get to the meet across the border and back to Bangkok with our load, you get a five hundred dollar bonus."

He looks at Henry and begins to laugh,"Damn boss you look like some old lady, how you do that?"

Henry just smiles,"Don't you worry about me load up those hay bales, some day I'll let you in on my secrets. Just keep your mouth shut and you will live a few years longer now move it we have to be at the Cambodian border before sunrise." It took three hours on Route 3 to reach the Cambodian border the sun was just rising over the horizon as they stopped at the guard shack, Harry sat in the rear of the truck wrapped in a shawl, the Border guard questioned Charn, only glanced at Henry dressed as an old woman in the truck bed. After a few questions waved them through. They traveled another twenty miles pulled over at a gas station and filled the tank. Henry's cell phone rang it was Carl,"Meet me a mile from the gas station and make it quick. I had to bribe half the country, these people sure know how to make a quick buck. I have ten kilos of heroin and quaaludes, I've contacted a couple of Brits that are willing to sneak it out of the country when we meet I'll give you their info."

Henry jumped into the truck,"Go one mile further on Route 3 and park, blink the headlights three times then shut off the engine." Charn pulled onto the berm of the highway, blinked the lights three times. They waited twenty minutes, a sedan pulled alongside the truck.Carl signaled Henry to come to the side of the car.

"Jesus Henry, I never know what your next disguise will be. That old lady getup is a show stopper.Ok, lets get the show on the road the drugs are in my trunk." They place the contraband in a false compartment under the truck bed.

Henry sprays the drugs with disinfectant, hopefully it will keep the dogs at the border from detecting the cargo. He seals the space with a metallic tape and spray paints the underside of the truck. Carl wants to get the hell out of there staying in one place too long will bring unneeded attention especially so close to the border. He has some of the authorities in his pocket but knows not to flaunt it.

Carl,"Henry, I have to get the hell out of here I don't need any crap from the local law, you have the merchandise, hand over my cut from the sale and I am gone."

Henry walks back to the truck and tells Charn,"Lift up the front seat and you will see a package, pick it up drop it on the side of the road, then back up pull into the trees and wait for me. We still have things to do before we head back to Bangkok. I want to wait till two o'clock tomorrow morning when everyone is half asleep."

Chapter Five

He slams the truck door picks up the package and walks back to Carl. Henry,"I need a favor my friend, where is the nearest house from here I haven't had a good piece in awhile, don't even begin to tell me you don't have any idea. You'r about as as perverted as they come."Carl retorts.

Carl,"There's a house thirty kilometers on Route 3, she will take care of all your needs and then some, I'll count the take when I get back to my place and it better all be there."

Henry snaps back,"Don't sweat the small shit, you get two thirds and I get a third, why would I try to stiff you, the CIA would love to get their hands on us. We are a good fit and as long as we work together we can make a good living. Have a good night, I will contact you in a couple of weeks as to the location of our next rendezvous."

Henry walked back to the truck, removed his disguise, dressed in his regular traveling clothes, climbed into the truck and motioned Charn to drive further into Cambodia.

Charn protests,"Hell boss where are we going? I thought we are heading back home my girlfriend is waiting for me."

Henry,"Just do as I ask, we have a few clicks to go I need to have some fun and what is this girlfriend bullshit. Here is your five hundred dollars so do as I ask and just drive. Henry,"I'll tell you when to stop."

They drove in silence Henry kept a lookout for the house,"Carl said it would be on the left just past a local store.Slow down Charn, what's with you, you'r acting strange."

Charn answers,"Nothing boss, I just don't feel good must be something I ate."

Henry looks at Charn he is sweating profusely, Henry begins to wonder what the hell is going on.Thinking back to when they stopped at the border, the guard appeared to recognize Charn and Charn gave him a nod of the head as if to say you don't know me. Henry,"This little creep is setting me up he has sold me out to the CIA or he is going to take me for the drugs and probably have me killed.Knowing I would have to be killed or turned over to the Authorities because if I was still able to function he would eventually die a very slow and painful death. Henry thought how he should handle the problem."Should I kill the little prick now or wait till we were at the whore house and how would I get the drugs into Thailand if I offed him. I think I'll let him play his hand and then make my decision."Henry spotted the Whore house,"This is the place pull in and shut off the motor, Charn you go in and see what it looks like, I'll be right behind you don't worry I will pick up the cost for the night."

Henry waited a couple of seconds then silently exited the truck, he could see Charn talking on his cell phone, he slipped into the shadows moving swiftly to Charn's left and rear so he could hear the conversion."We are about an hours drive from the border at a house of Pleasure on the left side of the road. The truck is parked in front I will keep him busy inside you take the truck I'll give him a lethal overdose to kill him, then we can take over his part in the drug trade, plus there is a wanted poster offering ten thousand dollars for his head dead or alive, I will expect you in two hours."

When he hung up Henry cracked him in the back of the head with a lug wrench from the truck, Charn groaned and fell to the ground like a sack of dirt, lifting the wrench to finish the job, hesitated, having second thoughts. He dragged Charn back to the truck and threw him into the truck bed and tied him up, went to the tool box opened the false bottom removed the drugs and hid them in the woods for safe keeping.

Henry calls Carl,"We have a big problem my driver tried to set me up and bogart the drugs how far are you from the House? Get your ass here "asap" his crew will be here in less than two hours." Carl,"I'll be there in less than forty minutes, I'm on my way."

Henry checked Charn he was barely breathing, dragged him out of the truck bed and placed him in the drivers seat tied his hands to the steering wheel, he cut the gas line and rigged it so when they tried to start the truck the leaking gas would ignite causing the gas tank to explode. He saw head lights in the distance coming toward him, it must be Carl.

Henry stepped into the shadows of the building he held the pistol against his left leg and waited till the truck came to a complete stop. The passenger door opened Henry watched as someone stepped out of the truck carrying a shotgun, the high beams on the truck partially blinded Henry, cocking the gun he could feel the sweat running down his forehead,"Goddamned sweat is ruining my aim."

He dropped on one knee and brought up the pistol,"Jesus Christ! Henry put that fucking thing down before you kill somebody." Henry,"Your late, the bastards tried to set me up grab the money and drugs, how do I know you weren't in on it." Carl straightened up and grimaced,"Give me a break, if I wanted you dead I'd do it my self, besides you are too valuable an asset."Carl exclaimed."I know they are looking for me in Thailand, I figured Cambodia would be safer." Carl,"Henry,Henry,Henry you can't keep away from the women, every time you blow a nut you have to beat the shit out of the whore. Your only saving grace is they can't put a true face on who or what you are. I've found an outlet for weapons and drugs, I need a strong right hand, somebody I can trust who isn't afraid to screw over our competition when they get out of line.You in or out."

Henry,"I'm in, now what?"

"Now take me for instance when I'm done I bury them in the back yard."Carl just smiles.

"We load the drugs on my truck and get the hell out of here, Charn's buddies will be here in about half an hour, we'll be on our way further into Cambodia when the truck blows.I never did trust that little son of a bitch" Carl answers laughing."They load the heroin, Henry climbs into the back seat of the truck. He still has his doubts about who tried to set him up and he wasn't taking any chances, the driver was one huge dude, stood six feet three, with arms like an ape, Carl introduced him,"Henry this is my bodyguard Gregory he's from the Caucus,I buy weapons from the Russian Mafia and he's my go between a really sweet guy if you don't cross him, because if you do he will rip your head off, won't you Greg my boy?"

Greg answers in a deep Russian accent,"You got it boss, I like ripping peoples heads off,Har, Har, me funny."

When they were further from the border Henry looked out the rear window and saw a bright flash, the truck he had rigged exploded. The fire ball could be seen for miles.

Forty miles into Cambodia the truck took a jungle path to evade the military patrols. After an hour the truck turned left they were back on the main road,"We're about an hours drive from the base, the local police have been paid off to look the other way, they get a cut of the take and are happy campers" Carl comments.

Chapter Six

Morrisons cell phone rings he picks up the call,"This is George we have a problem, Henry is in Cambodia, we had him marked for elimination somehow the slippery son of a bitch figured out that he was marked killed his driver and blew up the calvary. He and Carl disappeared into the jungle with the drugs and money. So now we have another problem the Russians are gun running along with bringing in Uzbek women as prostitutes illegally. The scuttlebutt is there will be a drop shipment of weapons this week somewhere along the coast, most likely the Patani region of Thailand. The Insurgents are attempting to make that area ungovernable.They want Autonomy and the separatists are not willing to negotiate, period! We have a satellite in place hopefully we will be able to perform an interdiction before the cargo is handed over to the BRN-C. I have been in communication with FBI Agent Jepson he has agreed to release Marjorie Swift from house arrest, she will be arriving in Bangkok Airport day after tomorrow."

Morrison,"George how did you pull off that one, Jepson wanted her to serve ten to twenty in Federal Prison, what in the hell did you promise him?" George,"Can't tell you over the phone we'll sit down over a scotch and I'll clue you in someday." Marjorie Swift back in the States had worn a hole in her living room rug, the sweat was running down her back. She had an entire Cross Fit layout in her basement, in order to release her pent up emotions had completed the last series of dead lifts of two hundred twenty pounds and climbed the rock wall till her hands were raw and bleeding, through the sweat and tears screamed in frustration thinking,"I wish that mousey FBI punk Jepson was here I would kick his skinny ass, who in the frigging does he think he is putting me under house arrest."

Marjorie Swift stripped naked, walked into the shower, turned on the cold water, she let it soothe her aching body, just as her skin started to turn blue switched it over to hot sliding down the shower wall letting the water run down her firm breasts and between her muscular thighs.

Marjorie,"God I need a good lay, I don't care if it's with a woman or a man."

After the shower she toweled off finishing with it between her legs, pulled her hair back letting it dry naturally, sprayed her body with perfume, climbed into a pair of tight shorts and halter, threw her bra on the bed and walked out of the bedroom thinking,"I sure as hell don't need that piece of hardware with my firm tits."

Her door bell ringing brings her back to reality,"Who in the hell is that?, could be somebody trying to sell me something, maybe I will punch the asshole in the jaw and get myself arrested, at least it will get me out of this stink hole.She screams," ALL RIGHT,... ALL RIGHT, I'M COMING!" Marjorie opened the door so hard it hit the hall wall.She stood there with a look of surprise on her face," I'll be a son of a bitch, God has answered my prayers." As she reached out with both hands to place them around Jepson's throat. He immediately stepped back before she could tighten her grip,"What the hell are you doing Miss Swift, control yourself are you nuts?"

She snapped out of her trance thinking,"Jesus this is real I almost strangled the creep, I don't need an attempted murder charge. Jepson what are you doing here I thought you and I were through, what in the hell do you want?"

FBI Agent Jepson,"Not my call, this comes from the Justice Department they have given me orders to remove your leg bracelet and release you from house arrest. With one condition you are to help Morrison in Thailand, he is on Harry and Carl's trail and needs your help. You can speak a number of mid eastern dialects and some Thai so I am told." Marjorie answers,"Sounds good to me, where's my pardon signed by the President and Attorney General of the United States.Then and only then, I'll do what ever they want." Jepson,"Jesus Marjorie, you haven't changed still a real bitch, I'll see what I can do."

Marjorie,"SCREW YOU! and the horse you rode in on, you know damned well they told you I would be pardoned, but no you are still playing your goddamned games. Now get your skinny ass off my steps before I break your neck and by the way take off my ankle bracelet before you leave and don't come back unless it's with the pardon."

He reaches down and removes the ankle bracelet, as he stands up Marjorie slams the door in his face.

Jepson,"Man what a bitch, no wonder she never got married, the poor bastard would probably have had a ring in his nose." Marjorie is swearing under her breath, then she starts to laugh hysterically,"I beat that little bastard, I beat him at his own game. I can't wait to see Morrison." She opens a bottle of whiskey and pours herself three fingers, sits on the couch siping the alcohol refills the glass relaxing as her eyes become heavy with sleep. The suns rays slipping through the window blinds wake her up. "What the, where am I? Shit I must have fallen asleep on the couch."

She heads to the bathroom spends a few minutes in the shower and towels off, pulled her hair into a pony tail, brushed her teeth, dresses and heads to the front door.She opens the door there stands an an FBI Agent.

"What in the hell are you doing here? Go help that boss of yours get my pardon, if you want to do something take me to the nearest Dojo. You have a problem with that?"

The Agent answers,"No Ma'am, anywhere you wish, do you want me to wait for you?"

She stepped back his… answer had taken her by surprise," If you wish I'll probably be a couple of hours."

The Agent escorts her to the car, the drive to the Dojo takes twenty minutes he parks the car,"I'll wait for you till you're done."

Marjorie enters the Dojo removes her shoes bowing to the Sensei,"Marjorie, long time no see, where have you been." "I guess you could say I was detained for a few months." Sensei,"What can I do for you?" She replies,"I would like to limber up and practice my karate and jujutsu is there anyone here I can practice with." Sensei smiles,"Promise not to break any bones, please." Marjorie grapples with a couple of the biggest students in the Dojo working up a sweat, she finally sits on the mat with a pleased look on her face."

CHAPTER SEVEN

Sensei,"How you feel Marjorie , you haven't lost your edge, I would be pleased if you could follow me into my office I have something to show you, Please." Marjorie follows the Sensei into his office."Please sit down, there have been a couple of nasty looking bulls looking for you I think they are Carl's men. So be careful the word on the street is you have a price on your head."She looks up," and how much am I worth to that scummy bastard."

"He answers,"Half a million he hates you with a vengeance, you ruined him in the states and now he has to hide in a breakwater country in Asia for the rest of his life." Marjorie,"The bastard is a homicidal maniac he killed at least a dozen young women and I am sure he hasn't changed his spots. I am going to track him down and cut off his balls and make him eat them before I put him out of humanity's misery." She stood up and bowed,"I thank you for warning me I will be on my guard."

Marjorie walks out of the Dojo, signals to the Agent she is ready to leave, he pulls the car over as she slides into the back seat something doesn't feel right." No need to sit back there you can sit up here with me Ma'am."

"That's ok, I'll sit here thanks, by the way what is your name I don't remember seeing you before."

My name is Adam,"I was assigned to you this morning for your protection." She countered,"you mean Agent Samuelson? He's the lead Agent in my case."

"Yes Ma'am, he said I am to protect you with my life." Marjorie noticed he only had one hand on the steering wheel the right hand was not visible,"the bastard is going to snuff me right here." On her exit from the

Dojo she had picked up a pair of nunchucks, she slid as far to the drivers left as possible and swung the nunchucks at the drivers right shoulder. The force of the blow caused the gun to discharge luckily the weapon was pointing away from her, she took a second snap of the nunchucks across his head, there was a sharp crack as the back of his skull opened up and he fell against the steering wheel. The car careened off the street smashing against the side of a building, Marjorie jumped from the car just as it was kissing the store front, she rolled and stood up,"I better get my ass to Thailand this neighborhood is too damned dangerous."

She took off running and when she reached her house called Jepson,"We have a problem some one is impersonating an FBI Agent he just tried to kill me. I need to get out of here tonight and be on my way to Thailand."

Jepson,"What in the hell are you talking about, I pulled my people last night." Marjorie,"Yea well, somebody is out to kill me and I think it's Carl, somehow he knows I'm on my way to Thailand."

Jepson,"give me an hour maybe I can find you a seat on a CIA flight. They have a secret airfield in LA in the meantime I will send an armored car to pick you up."

As Marjorie was hanging up she heard a ominous click,"The bastards have tapped my phone. In an hour I will be dead meat." She walked down the cellar stairs, removed the lock on a steel door, reviewing the array of weapons at her command. She picked the hand held M4 Assault Rifle and a Glock 19, loaded up with armor piercing ammo. Closed and locked the vault, pulled the light switch a door slid open to a tunnel that led under the street at the rear of the house, as she exited the basement it activated the laser system that when the beams were broken would in sixty seconds cause the house to implode. Marjorie,"I have to get the hell out of the blast zone, I figure they will be kicking in the door in about ten minutes, the tunnel ended a block away she climbed the ladder that exited into the middle of an inner alley way, the garage door slid open she walked to her bike," There's my baby when I open her up she'll do at least one hundred and twenty an hour. I need to move if I know anything they are throwing flash bangs and tear gas through my windows as I speak. I give them five minutes and my door will be ripped off the hinges, their thermal imaging camera will lead to a heat source on the second floor reading 98.6 degrees.

That would be my doppelgänger and in sixty seconds everything will go boom." Marjorie zipped up her blast jacket, donned her helmet, laid the M4 across the handle bars and took the first corner doing eighty, on the straight away punched it to one hundred miles an hour."Come on baby, Marjorie needs to put miles between me and the Death Squad."Looking behind her spots a Police Car pull out of an alley with it's lights and siren blaring.Just as she was about to try to loose the Police there was a tremendous explosion, the blast waves broke windows half a mile away. The pursuing Police did a one eighty heading back toward the blast."Holy shit, maybe I used too much C4, only wanted to drop the house not the entire neighborhood." Marjorie chuckled.

Chapter Eight

She took the back roads trying to find the runway, she texted Jepson,"Where in the hell is the CIA runway?"

"One mile past the main terminal there is a dirt road turn left and travel two miles, you will see a hanger they are waiting for you."Jepson texts.

As she drives toward the hanger two men exit with machine guns pointed at the windshield of her bike, she jams on the brakes coming to a screeching halt."Get off the bike now, keep your hands where we can see them." The scruffy Agent hollers.She dismounts slowly pushing the kick stand in place keeping her hands where they can be seen places both her hands on top of her head."My name is Marjorie Swift FBI Agent Jepson has talked to the CIA and I have a seat on this flight to Bangkok,Thailand." she answers, before the Agents can question her."They ask,"Who is your contact in Thailand?" Marjorie answers,"CIA Agent George Wilson and Lieutenant Morrison of the LA Police Department. They have requested my assistance in apprehending the fugitives Henry and Carl." The two men look at each other, Mike pulls out a picture of Marjorie,"Sure as hell looks like her, Please drop your bags on the ground and take off the coat she places the Glock and M4 on the ground,"Frisk her to make sure she isn't carrying any concealed weapons."

Mike does a thorough pat down."She's clean, nothing in the bag or coat."

CIA Agent,"OK, you can board in fifteen minutes we will be airborne in the hour. Marjorie boards the plane takes a seat towards the front near the pilots cabin, she looks around the back half of the plane the seats have been removed and there are crates of weapons and ordinance,She thinks to herself,"This plane has enough firepower to start a Third World War." all of a sudden she hears her name, "Jesus, Marjorie Swift where have you been, so your the one they called up to help in the investigation. I heard Carl has a price on your head, you really twisted his balls in LA too bad you didn't finish him off." She turns around in the seat,"I'll be a son of a bitch Johnny last I heard you had a desk job in DC."

Johnny,"I couldn't take it the politics are suffocating I had to get back in the field so I could breath.You mind if I sit here." she answers,"Hell no sit, are you going to be part of the team in Thailand?" Johnny quips,"So I'm told, The Thai Government has a number of ongoing problems,

There is a militant uprising in the south, the Russians and Chinese are selling weapons to the militants, bringing in drugs and Uzbek women and young girls are being forced into illegal prostitution and Henry and Carl are involved in the operation. We estimated they are pulling down at least a couple million a month." Marjorie answers,"and as long as they are operating out of Cambodia and Laos they cannot be extradited. So we have to make it worth their while to cross the border into Thailand, what does the CIA have in mind?" "When we arrive in Bangkok I'll let Charley bring you up to date right now none of us has the need to know" Johnny smiles. She turns and looks out the window, the sound of the planes wheels locking into place for the landing wakes her out of her sleep."Damn, I slept through the entire flight, better drag my ass to the washroom clean up and throw some water on my face."

The plane circled Bangkok and headed west to a private air strip twenty miles from the city. After they deplaned everyone was ushered into the hanger and told to take a seat. The Section Chief Charley Wilson starts the briefing,"I will give everyone their assignments, but first I want to make a major point, there will be Thai Officials made privy to our objectives. So be that it may, I want to compartmentalize this operation. Marjorie and Johnny you two are to work with Lieutenant Morrison. I want you gone before the Thai's arrive.

There's a car outside the driver will take you to your safe house." Marjorie and Johnny were given their orders and exited the hanger."What in the hell is going on?" Marjorie asked.

Johnny,"I think Charlie doesn't want to expose our entire operation, he feels that the Thai's may have a mole but he hasn't quite figured out who it is."

Marjorie thinks,"That's nice we haven't even got the operation off the ground and Charley already smells a rat." A-Wat opens the car door for Marjorie, Johnny jumps in the front seat ,"OK mate, lets get this bucket on the road, just call me Johnny and that beautiful bird in the back is Marjorie. By the way what's your name?"

My name A-Wat I work for Lieutenant Morrison and Charley, what ever you need I am at your service.They good people." Marjorie leans over the seat and asks,"How far to the safe house?" A-Wat,"About thirty klicks not that far, Morrison said for me to tell you act like tourists the hotel is crawling with Russians." They sit back and enjoy the ride the car pulls up to the Bangkok Hotel."Please wait in Hotel lobby while I remove your luggage from the car and pick up your room key." They walked into the hotel arm in arm giggling and laughing,Johnny scanned the lobby and bar for un-friendlies sitting at the bar were two Russians drinking water glasses of Russian Vodka, they were half plastered hustling bar maid. Johnny whispers into Marjorie's ear,"Your nine o'clock we need to keep a close eye out for those boys."

They are built like bulls and probably just as mean."

She just shakes her head and smiles,"Better follow our guide he's heading for the elevator."

Meanwhile at the bar,"Hey Ivan you see that blond I think I try to put my meat in her." Ivan responds,"The boss told you to keep out of trouble, we have a shipment tonight and Sergi you'r not to screw things up."

Sergi,"Ok,Ok I be good boy but after we deliver the shipment I want to party. You got problem with that?" Ivan just shakes his head,"After we do a job on the CIA up stairs, we Party."

Sergei hollers to the bartender,"Hey bring me a bottle of vodka and put it on the bar with two glasses, we going to party." The bartender hesitates he looks at the manager sitting at a table in the bar area. The manager says,"Give them what they want just put it on their tab."

It was a long, hard night.

Chapter Nine

The phone rings,"Charlie, we're in the lobby, I just overheard the Russians talking at the bar, they have your suite bugged I don't know how, but they are setting us up for a take down you should begin breaking down the equipment now. It appears we have a turn coat ,sign 776." He puts down the phone and dials Morrison,"Morrison we have a breach, call the rest of the crew we need to move "asap."

Morrison contacts Marjorie, Johnny and A-Wat,"Code Red, Code Red everybody be at Charlies Suite in fifteen minutes." Meanwhile Charley had all the files loaded and surveillance equipment ready to go, when the rest of the team arrived.

George Wilson,"A-Wat where is the van." A-Wat,"In the alley running, where we going boss?" Wilson,"Johnny has the new safe location, Marjorie and Morrison you two take point, drive the black SUV it's armored." A-Wat,"Johnny lets get this equipment out of here take the freight elevator." Charley hands everyone in the crew a Glock 19 with a dozen full clips each. Morrison,"Marjorie your with me, there is automatic weapons in the SUV, and armored vests. If the Russians are smart they probably hired one of the Bangkok street gangs to ambush us, they could care less about the local authorities the gangs act with impunity. They pay off the local Police to look the other way."

The elevator door opens at the lower level. Morrison and Marjorie cautiously exit the elevator. Morrison warns Marjorie to block the entrance to the hotel, he opens the exit door to the street, surveys the area it appears to be clear, starts the SUV remotely and drives it across the door way giving them cover from unfriendly fire.

A-Wat taps Morrison on the shoulder,"I go for the van."

Morrison,"Wait till I check out the street, this could be a setup and you would be walking into an ambush." He scanned the area through the snipers scope on the M4 assault rifle. "I'll be a son of a bitch, there's a half a dozen shooters behind those dumpsters. You would have been mince meat."

Marjorie hollers to Morrison,"Call Charley and tell him to stop scratching his balls we are surrounded, it looks like the Russians are one step ahead of us, bring the essentials and destroy everything else."

His phone rings twice,"What's the problem?" Morrison answers,"Five more minutes and we are dust, destroy everything and get your butt down here." Charley slams down the phone,"Johnny throw everything in a pile, pour acid on it and we are out of here."

Charley and Johnny tumbled out of the elevator, Morrison holds the exterior door to the rear of the hotel open as the crew escapes into the SUV. Morrison leans the M4 against the top of the car and fires a grenade at the van and then at the gang's chase car. The van exploded in a fire ball lifting the truck into the air sending it flying into a row of stores, the occupants of the chase car disappeared into the shadows before the second grenade could be fired, it struck the car midships and it disintegrated into a blazing pile of twisted metal.

Morrison jumps into the passengers seat,"Lets get the hell out of here, head for the airstrip." Marjorie starts to laugh,"Hell Morrison, you haven't changed your still a tight ass giving orders" before Morrison can answer.

A-Wat asks,"We leaving Thailand boss?,I have family here." He answers,"No we are going to the bunker to regroup and evaluate our options."

Charley Wright calls the base,"Enemy in the wire, enemy in the wire, have the C 17 ready to accept cargo we are going to the bunker, call sign CW 777, do you copy, do you copy?" The base replies,"We copy boss, we copy CW 777 everything will be ready and waiting what is your ETA?" Charley answers,"ETA two hours."

Marjorie keeps watch to make sure they don't get bush whacked, they could have snipers along the road out of Bangkok. They were an hour out of Bangkok so far, so good, then she spots the reflection from a snipers rifle,"Son of a bitch, everyone close the windows we have hostiles at one o'clock, lock and load lets hope they don't have RPG's or we can kiss our asses goodby." She hollers to Johnny hand me the M4 with the scope, and open the roof. I'm taking the sniper out before he has us in his sights." Marjorie lays the M4 on the top of the SUV and waits for the target to show, slowly sticks her head out of the sun roof and fires. In slow motion they see the snipers head explode as he tumbles down the hill like a bag of rags."Charley, Johnny we need to saturate the hill with grenades, hand a few up here and lets clear the area of hostiles." They blast the hill with grenades, all movement ceases,"A-Wat kick this thing in the ass we need to get to the air strip now."A few miles past the encounter Morrison hollers,"Stop the car this is open ground I need to check for a tracking device, how in the hell did they know what road we were taking and everybody check their clothes and wallets I think we have been set up.We could be leading them to the base." Morrison jumps out of the SUV and activates his portable bug detector, Marjorie and Johnny follow right behind giving him cover. As he walks around the car the detector lights up like a Christmas tree, he sweeps Marjorie and Johnny and they are bugged too."I'll be damned we have been betrayed." He looks at A-Wat sitting behind the wheel," That little creep is the only one who had access to our living quarters, luggage and transportation.

A-Wat keep your hands where I can see them and climb out of the car now." The blood drains from A-Wats face as he slowly exits the SUV," Boss please don't kill me I have no choice, they threaten to kill my family."

Morrison,"What's that tattoo on your arm? It looks familiar push up you sleeve so I can get a better look." A-Wat slowly pushes up his sleeve. "That's a gang tattoo the same as the sniper we just took out. What's your game A-Wat are you working for the Russians or the Chinese, I should put a bullet in your lying head and leave your dead ass in the bush for playing both sides of the fence."Morrison threatens sarcastically.

Morrison,"I will ask you one more time, who are you working for?"

A-Wat drops to his knees,"Please don't kill me I'm being paid by the Chinese, they paid me to spy on what the CIA was planning. The Chinese Military are involved with a couple of Americans who are going to deliver weapons to the insurgents in the south of Thailand that are being financed by the Chinese. The Russians are more into drugs and prostitution."Morrison,"Why in the hell are the Chinese selling arms to the Insurgents in the south, what do they hope to accomplish?"

Agent,"They want to destabilize the southern area, and force the Thai Government into asking for Chinese assistance to quell the rebellion, once they have troops employed in Thailand the troops will be here permanently." A-Wat answers. Morrison thinks,"This little prick is more than he seems, I wouldn't be surprised if he is a double agent. The only problem is who's side is he really working for?" He turns slowly and points his pistol at A-Wats head, A-Wat stares directly into the gun barrel and doesn't even blink. The bastard is darling me to shoot,"You no shoot me boss, I have intelligence you will need to capture Henry and Carl. That is the main reason you are here!" Morrison retorts,"How in the hell do you know my reasons for being in Thailand?" A-Wat just smiles,"Ok, just get back in the car you sit in the passenger seat I will drive."They walk back to the car Morrison calls to Johnny," Shake our friend down make sure he doesn't have any weapons." Johnny,"Put both hands on the hood of the car and spread your legs." A-Wat does as he is told. Johnny finds a knife attached to a holster and a small pistol. Johnny looks at Morrison with a questioning glance as if to ask what now?

Morrison,"Put him in the seat next to me and you keep an eye on him for the rest of the ride. If he even looks like he is about to try something shoot him. Marjorie you take point, keep a lookout for any hostiles keep your head down that blond hair of yours makes a perfect target, Charley how you doing I don't need you to bleed out on me." "I'm Ok, the bullet just grazed me, lets get the hell out of here before they regroup and level us." Morrison steps on the gas leaving a cloud of dust in his wake, an hour later they arrive at the CIA site. Morrison blinks the car lights to let the agents know that they are friendlies.

He looks up a sniper on the roof wave them in, the doors to the hanger open and allow the car to park. They all get out of the car and stretch their legs. Charley walks over to the pilot,"We have been compromised, destroy all un-necessary files and set the destruct sequence for the building. I'll start the timer once we are in the air."

Chapter Six

All the files were shredded and burned, shape charges were checked a second time. The operator on the ground radar spotted activity approximately twenty miles from the site.

CIA Agent,"We have hostiles about half an hour coming fast, we need to get the hell out of here."

It only took the crew to board the Dash 8,Q300 about twenty minutes, by luck the landing strip was ninety degrees from the incoming enemy. The hanger doors opened the plane taxied out onto the ramp and the pilot kicked it in the ass. The planes wheels were up and locked when they were at the end of the twenty five hundred foot strip.Charley hollered to the pilot," Turn due west that will put us out of the line of fire and point the nose up till we are at least thirty thousand feet." Charley started the countdown it would take sixty seconds and the hanger would be gone.

Looking out the cabin window Marjorie could see the Hostiles entering the hanger, one of them pointed what looked to be a surface to air missile toward the plane, before the hostile with the Launcher could fire the hanger disappeared in a huge explosion, and the enemy evaporated in the blast. "Jesus" Marjorie explained,"They never had a chance."

Charley just laughed,"Those bastards had it coming our next stop is a safe house in Cambodia." The pilot turns to Morrison,"We have permission to land at the airport in Phnom Penh, arrival time forty five minutes, we have a safe house twenty miles outside of the city." The plane lands immediately taxies into a hanger with the door closing behind them."Ok people we need to get to the house and set up asap, there is a lot of work to be done in the next twenty four hours." The equipment was loaded into a pick up truck and the other SUV's were used to transport the rest of the crew. They arrived at midnight and started to set up their monitoring equipment and external cameras, logged into the centers main frame in DC and confirming their location. Charley called the crew together to give everyone instructions as to what their targets would be.

"Morrison I want you and Marjorie to scout Carl's compound and see how vulnerable they are, Johnny you and Mike monitor the phone lines and computers, we have to have a handle on when the weapons shipment is going to be picked up by Carl and Henry." Morrison and Marjorie put on their bullet proof vests, checked their weapons and loaded enough ammo for a fire fight in case they were spotted by guards at the compound. (Meanwhile at the Drug Compound in Cambodia)

Henry was having a shit fit,"I thought you said I would have a 3-D printer here this morning Carl?"Carl smirks, "Henry you are one twisted son of a bitch, all you think of is getting your rocks off. Relax it will be here at the end of the week."

Henry,"Want the 3-D printer for a disguise, I told you a couple of days ago we are being watched. There was a tourist outside of the compound taking pictures and he was a tourist like I am, the CIA is setting us up for a fall." Carl answers,"We're in Cambodia they can't touch us." "Bullshit they took out that guy in Pakistan in the middle of the night with Seal Team six. If they want us real bad the CIA will do what ever is necessary."

Henry shook his head and went to his quarters thinking, "What can I use to disguise myself?" He opened his suitcase there was a black wig, went into the bathroom and opened a jar of gelatin, mixed it with glycerine poured in just enough water the mix would thicken added skin color and applied it to the left side of his face as it was drying he added a red dye when he was done the left side of his face looked as if he had third degree burns. He then applied ground coffee to the rest of his skin to simulate dirt as if he hadn't washed in quite awhile.When the disguise was complete Harry looked in the mirror smiling,"I haven't lost my touch." Henry left his apartment and walked toward the escape tunnel. He heard the click of a gun being cocked."Who in the hell are you, what are you doing in my compound?" Yells Carl. Henry turns to face Carl with his hands in the air," Holy shit Carl it's me Henry get that frigging gun out of my face" Henry yells.

"Damn,Henry you have to let me know when you go native.I almost shot you, I thought you were an intruder."

"I told you I was going to recon the Compound, we are being watched. If I'm correct be ready to move tonight when I return."

Henry opened the hatch leading to the escape tunnel. After twenty minutes he emerged in a thicket of palm trees.After walking away from the compound for twenty minutes he turned left onto the road that led back to the compound, walking slowly leaning on a cane and limping.

Marjorie was posted on the roof of a building two blocks away, she was watching who arrived and left the compound. The man walking with the cane caught her eye she put her glasses on him and shuttered as she drops the glasses,"That poor bastard had the left side of his face scarred, it looked like an acid burn." Henry sits on the curb in front of the compound in order to better survey the buildings. He sees the glare of a scope on the building directly down the street."I'll be a son of a bitch they are keeping surveillance on us, they know where we are and I would bet that we will get a visit in the next twenty four hours." Standing up and leaning on his cane walks slowly back down the street, as soon as he passes the rear of the compound turns into the woods and travels back to the hidden tunnel, a few minutes later he enters the house,"Carl, Carl where in the hell are you I told you we were being watched." Carl was laying on his bed just finishing up with a prostitute,"Who in the hell is calling my name? It better be something worth while of I'll cut your balls off."Carl walks out into the hall naked his belly roll almost covers his manhood standing holding a glass of whiskey. "Damned Carl, that is the last thing I wanted to see is your dick. Put on a pair of pants you'r not my type."He answers as he turns to re-enter the bedroom,"Screw you Harry you are no fashion model."Carl walks back into the hall wearing a pair shorts, "What's so damned important?"

Henry says,"There is a spotter one block over I saw the glare on the scope, I would bet they will be moving on us in less than twenty four hours, probably later tonight."

Marjorie sits on the roof thinking about what she had just seen,"I would swear that was Henry the way he walked but the face, Morrison said he was a master at disguises. I better contact the crew we may have to move sooner than planned." She calls the safe house after one ring the phone is answered,"Hello who is this?" Marjorie answers,"We have a problem tell Morrison or Charley we have to move tonight I think we have been spotted."

Johnny,"Ok I'll make sure they get the message." the person on the other end hangs up. She looks at the phone quizzically,"What the hell was that, did I call the wrong number?"Johnny has a smile on his face as he sets the phone in the charger,"See you in hell bitch."

Chapter Seven

The phone rings at the compound Carl picks up,"I told you not to contact me unless it's an emergency, what's that you say, how many?Twenty with the Americans, when tonight?" "Henry we have to move now, see if we can take out that spotter. Send four men, we have to neutralize the lookout, In the mean time I'll get our men in place to keep the CIA busy while we get away."

Henry called Arun,"We are being watched by someone on the roof across the street you need to kill the bastard, take four men and and don't come back till the job is done." "Will do boss no problem."The hit squad slipped out the back door, circling the block to take out Marjorie, before she realized what was happening.

Marjorie was getting nervous, she went to the back of the building noticed mens shadows carrying machine guns sneaking around the back through an alley way.

Marjorie,"I am screwed, that was Henry and I had a chance to take him out, he must have spotted me. Now there are at least four hostiles looking to snuff me." She had two grenades and plenty of ammo, she had to take them out or at least put them on the offensive so she could escape, of course this would definitely alert the enemy and the attack on the Compound would be almost impossible without casualties."These bastards have me between a rock and a hard place. It's up to Charley and Morrison, but I would abort the attack and wait them out."

She slowly leans over the parapet of the building, pulls the pin on the grenade and drops it in front of the gunmen, then drops the second grenade in back of them. Ducks down and covers her head, the concussion from the grenades rocks the rear of the building, looking through an opening in the parapet, there are three men down, one is staggering and out of nowhere someone opens up with a machine gun. "I'll be a son of a bitch there's still a live one looking to kill me." She decides to run for it, there may be who knows how many she would have to take on, and her chances of survival would be nil to zero, taking Marjorie jumps over the roof and lands on a overhanging canopy rolls onto the street heads for her car. It starts and as she is driving away tires squealing, there is a burst of gunfire from the roof. The shooter misses and Marjorie is hell bent to warn the rest of the crew at the safe house.

Morrison asks Johnny,"Have you heard from Marjorie she was supposed to call in at 2:30 and it's 3 O'clock, It's not like her?" Haven't heard a thing I'd let you know, I'll go to the site and see If she is alright." He runs down the stairs, starts the SUV and takes off.Morrison smells a rat and hollers to Charley,"Did you vet Johnny before he left the states? he's acting strange."

Charley answers,"Funny you ask I just had a wire from the office they found a body in the rest room of the airport and they think it is our man, put that punk under arrest." "No can do, he just screwed out of here in a hell of a hurry,I think we better warn Marjorie we have a mole and the name is Johnny." Morrison dials Marjorie,"Watch out for Johnny he is a plant.Probably coming your way beware."

She looks at her phone,"He was probably the prick who answered my call and left me to die. Maybe I can return the favor." Coming down the street is Johnny in the SUV, he waves to Marjorie to pull over, she places her automatic in her lap and slows down. He rolls down his window and smiles as he pulls along side of the car." Marjorie your ok, that's good Morrison is looking for you" at that moment he raises his gun to put a bullet in her head, she has her automatic cocked and ready, before he can fire she raises her gun and empties all twelve rounds through his open window, Johnny's head explodes the bullets leave a headless corpse, there is blood squirting everywhere. The SUV careens onto the curb and flips over exploding in a fire ball, the drivers door springs open leaving a headless corpse laying still on the street. She looks back,"Sorry Johnny or whatever your name is don't have time to chat I have a meeting." Morrison watches as Marjorie pulls up to the Safe House quickly exits the car.She sprints in the front door,"Morrison we have to abort the mission they know everything. We will get our asses shot off, I am sure they are planning to ambush us." Morrison,"Calm down, calm down we have already revised our plans to take out Carl and Henry, what in the hell happened out there."

Marjorie answers,"I was spotted by Henry I didn't recognize the little frog till it was too late, he was disguised and before I realized it he was too far away to take out.The pecker head sent his men to kill me but I outsmarted them and escaped, that compound is a fortress it would be suicide to try and take it."

"So, did you see Johnny on your way back here?"Morrison asks. She smiles and points her finger in the form of a gun "bang, bang" that mouse is headless, that son of a bitch tried to waylay me. I gave him a headache he will never forget" she started to laugh.

"So I take it, we won't have to worry about him in the future." Marjorie smiles," You got it brother not ever again on this green earth."

Charley calls to the crew,"Everybody come here the satellite will be over the Compound in fifteen minutes. That will give us eyes on what they are doing, my guess is they are planning to move the weapons south toward the coast and rendezvous with the Insurgents near Pattani, Thailand that's where the Thai government is having the most push back from the rebels."

Morrison asks,"Why don't we laser the Compound and drop ordinance on the frigging place all that would be left would be a hole in the ground." Charley turns to Morrison and answers,"I don't think the Cambodian government would be to happy with us, number one we are not even supposed to be here and number two this area is densely populated we would take out a couple of hundred civilians and cause a international incident."

Chapter Eight

Henry,"Come on Carl get the finger out of your ass we have to move, I wouldn't put it past the CIA to target the Compound and have a drone drop a bomb on us that would leave a very large hole in the ground. Then claim we accidentally blew ourselves up."

Carl,"You have a point, it would take a major fire fight to take this Compound and I'm sure the CIA isn't willing to take multiple casualties." We need to keep them off balance,

"Arun take half a dozen men to the CIA safe house and keep them busy while we move the weapons.We'll meet you at the boat tonight."

Arun answers,"You got it boss I take those white eyes out permanently, they kill my brothers."Meanwhile at the safe house Marjorie looks at Charlie and Morrison,"We have a target on our backs, I'll bet Johnny boy revealed our location and If I was Carl I would be setting us up for an ambush, as I speak. We need to get the hell out of here and set up defensive positions." Charley,"You are quick, I have the house wired with C4. We moved the equipment out an hour ago, the team is set up across the street so we would catch them in a cross fire from two sides of the building, the armored SUV is waiting for us in the back so let's move." They all climbed into the SUV and Marjorie drove,"Let's go sweetheart, head back to the airport Mike will take care of the hostiles." Charley laughs. Marjorie floors the SUV and never looking back, she can imagine the upcoming fire fight thinking,"I sure would have liked to be there when they ambush those bastards." Mike the squad leader has his men set up three M249(SAW)

in a cross fire he sets up one machine gun in the building across the street, one in the alley way and the third on the left side of the safe house,"I want every one to hold fire till I give the signal, they need to be in our line of fire so we can push them into the building and blow it.

Everyone understand." The men just shake their heads yes. The sound of a truck approaching the house is coming closer the truck stops just short of the ambush, the hostiles leave the truck and silently approach the target Mike counts about fifteen to twenty."Hold your fire,I say hold their fire, wait till the first shot",Mike orders.

Finally after the hostiles reconnoitered the building moving into the kill zone.Mike fires the first salvo with the other shooters immediately following, in the first salvo five attackers are killed where they stand, the other half attempt to retreat to their vehicles the rest sprint for the house.

A grenade is launched from the alley way that destroys the terrorists truck, leaving the retreating attackers totally without cover, they are cut down in withering fire. The hostiles break into the house and use it as cover. Mike ready's to destroy the building, around the corner appears a number of women with their children on bicycles, He signals to cease fire and waves them away from the building,"Shit, if I blow the house it is liable to take out innocent civilians." He calls to the rest of the squad,"Let them escape we can't afford to take the innocents." The squad lightens up on the attackers allowing them to escape out the back of the building. Mike,"Lets roll it up we need to get the HELL out of here now, the HUMVEE crashes out of the woods, the crew climbs in scooting out of the fire zone.

One of the crew,"Sure would have liked to clean that entire bunch of scum off the face of the earth, but Mike is right we don't kill civilians."

Marjorie, Charlie and Morrison were waiting at the hanger the plane had taxied out and was waiting for the rest of the crew. "Lets go, hurry, hurry we have to be in Pattani, Thailand they are going to try to deliver the weapons tonight."

Morrison looks at Charley,"How are you so sure." Charley looks at Morrison and raises his eyebrows,"Come on my boy how do you think, I have an embed in their organization." The plane lands twenty miles from Pattani,"Ok, this is the plan we are to meet with a company of Thai special ops at midnight, there is a spy in the sky watching the boat carrying the weapons.We want to allow the weapons to be handed over to the Insurgents, the Thai government hasn't been able to identify who they are so the plan is two fold. The Thai's want the Insurgents and we want Carl and Henry we can legally arrest them on Thai soil.Marjorie you are to be our liaison you speak perfect Thai.We all need to have our faces concealed and wear armor because it probably will get nasty tonight. Anyone have questions?"

The Thai Special Ops were waiting in armored vehicles, the crew walks over to the waiting Thai troops.

Charlie,"Major my name is Charley Watson and this is my crew, we have been designated as observers by your government and the USA, is there anything we can do to help complete the mission?"

The Major bows Charley returns the greeting and then they shake hands,"Major Kiet I didn't recognize you in the dark, long time no see, do you have the coordinates as to where the boat will land, what can we do to help?"

Major Kiet,"If you could send two of your people acting as tourists in town maybe go to local restaurant get a feel for the general atmosphere. The locals usually have a feeling if something is up."

Charley calls over Mike and Marjorie,"You two bicycle into Pattani, scout around see if the streets are active or sparse, maybe have a meal, Marjorie you speak Thai ask if things have calmed down or are the insurgents active, maybe the waiter or waitress will spill their guts."Marjorie,"Come on Mike lets go the shipment is due in a couple of hours, hop on the bike and lets start pedaling." The trip took twenty minutes they looked for a restaurant,"Over there the Pantai Restaurant it looks promising." The bike was parked, they walked into the restaurant there were only half a dozen customers, Marjorie and Mike sat at an empty table and motioned to the waitress.They watched as she walked over to them, her hands were shaking as she placed the menus on the table, Marjorie placed her hand on the waitresses and asked in Thai,"You look tired child is something the matter?" The waitress answered no, nothing is the matter."

Marjorie persisted,"You look scared, where are all the customers tonight is it normally this quiet?"

The waitress whispered,"Insurgents threaten to kill tourists tonight, everyone stay home."

Marjorie smiles,"I'll have a bowl of Tom yum and the Green Papaya Salad, make mine the Red Curry with duck," Mike tells the waitress. We are hungry so if you can ask the chef to please put us first we would be very grateful."

Mike stood up and walked to the front entrance, he lit a cigarette all the while scanning the street for activity. The entire street was almost empty,"I wonder if they know the Thai military is just a couple of miles away and are setting us up for an ambush or engage in a fire fight to keep us occupied while the shipment changes hands?"

He turns and walks back to the table Marjorie gives him a quizzical look, while she is eating the Papaya Salad, "What's up Mike you look perplexed?" I think we are being set up. The Insurgents they are going to start some sort of counter move to keep the Thai troops engaged while the arms are off loaded and give Carl and Henry a chance to slip through our fingers and retreat back into Cambodia." Marjorie is sitting facing the window,"I'll be a son of a bitch there's someone walking this way I just saw his shadow, they may have made us when we biked into town. You carrying Mike?" Mike answers,"Hell yes!"Marjorie walks to the rear of the store looking for a way to exit. She calls Morrison,"This is a set up they know the Thai military is here and I think we were spotted. They are going to start a secondary action to lure you away from the objective so they can unload the weapons and keep you occupied trying to rescue us, hopefully there is only a handful, Mike and I can handle them if not I'll call for help."

Mike,"Lets go Marge before the bastards figure that out we're exiting out the back of the restaurant."

Mike checked to make sure the alley was empty,"Come on the alley is clear, we'll have to make a run for it." They ran for the woods and hid behind a stone wall,Marjorie dials her cell phone,"Charley warn Major Kiet they may be walking into an ambush, there is a lot of enemy activity. I have a feeling that they will engage the troops to keep them busy" just as she spoke there was gun fire.

She looked at Mike,"Holy shit our people are under attack I heard gun fire over the phone, we have to get back to the site." They took off running. The Insurgents that were stalking them had disappeared,"Marjorie,"We are all being played, I would bet my eye teeth that the they have maybe at best a half a dozen snipers keeping the entire contingent pinned down while the main body is off unloading the guns." Major Kiet was standing in the middle of the fire fight screaming orders,"Everybody form a perimeter and keep your heads down, bring up the armored car and level that patch of woods." The Armored car has a MK-19 Grenade machine gun the Major orders the trooper to open fire and not stop till the enemy fire is totally suppressed, you Lieutenant send three men with M110 sniper rifles with suppressors and flank the bastards I don't want to take any live prisoners, if they are still breathing put a bullet in their heads."

"Charley calls the Major over,"Major can I speak to you for a minute," What in the hell do you want I have a job to do."He answers."Please listen to me, I don't give a shit if you kill them, but wouldn't it be wise to let a couple of them live maybe you can get some intel out of the scum." He stands looking at Charley for a couple of minutes and starts to laugh,"Ok Charley, you are right I was all caught up in destroying the enemy." Major Kiet calls to his men, "Belay that order I need a couple of them alive so we can find out what they know but kill the rest of them."

CHAPTER NINE

The compound two days earlier,"Carl they should have wiped out those agents by now where in the hell are they?" Henry asks.Carl," I don't have a clue." He picks up the phone and calls Arun,"Arun where in the hell are you, did you finish them off?" the phone rang a number of times but it was not answered. Carl looks at the phone and shakes his head,"I'm tired of this shit" throws the phone across the room it hits the wall and the broken pieces scatter across the hallway."Jesus Christ, do I have to do everything where is that asshole?" Henry's phone rings,"Hello, who is this? it's Arun I tried to call Carl but no answer." Henry hands his phone to Carl,"Where are you, did you complete the mission?" There was a long pause on the other end,"No boss…., they were waiting for us they had us in a box and killed all but two of our men and destroyed the trucks, I think Johnny has been taken out a witness said a blond haired woman killed him in a gun fight.I found an overturned SUV with a headless body laying in the street, clothes look like him, but his head is gone."

Carl throws Henry's phone on the floor and starts to jump up and down on it crushing the phone into dust and screams,"She's done it again, that fucking bitch keeps screwing me over, she tries to kill me and now blows away my mole, she kills my men and walks away." He pulls his hair out in clumps and starts to cry,"I have to kill her, track her down like a dog, a rabid dog make her pay, he "SOBS" God I hate her."

Henry looks at Carl thinking," He has a screw loose, this Marjorie is so far up his ass he can't think straight."Henry reaches out and taps Carl on the shoulder, "Carl calm down, your not thinking straight we have a million dollar delivery to make in less than forty eight hours, have a drink, sniff some coke don't screw this up or we will have the Chinese looking to waste us."

Carl sits down on the couch, Henry pours him a full glass of scotch, opens a packet of coke makes two lines so he can snort it." He calms down, gulps the water glass of scotch, pulls out his straw and snorts two lines of coke lays back on the couch and sighs,"Henry, I hate her some day I will have my revenge." Henry replies,"Pull your self together, enough of this shit we have money to make, your day will come. Now lets figure how we get those weapons to the insurgents, we meet with the Cartel tonight and pick up five hundred thousand as a down payment the rest upon delivery."

There was a knock on the back door of the compound,"Who in the hell is that?, come in I don't have time to screw around." It's me boss Arun and my men, we were decimated it was a bloodbath." Carl didn't say a word he just turned around walked into the sitting room and slumped into a chair."Arun, do you know if they are aware of our delivery in a couple of days?, because if they are we will have to push up the delivery." Henry quizzes. Arn,"I don't know boss all I heard is they were leaving the area because it was too hot for them to do their work.Their safe house is booby trapped with C4 and It can be blown whenever they want." Henry,"See if you can round up another dozen men for tonight, arm them with machine guns. We have to meet with the Cartel tonight you have to pick up the weapons, then proceed south to the coast, load them on a waiting boat sail south to the Thai coast, any questions?" He bows and calls to the two survivors come with me I have to round up more men for tonight, go to the village and tell them they will be paid a months wages for two days work. Don't come back unless you can recruit at least a dozen men, now GO, GO!"

An hour later Henry looks out the upstairs window and sees about a dozen or more men gathering in the courtyard."

He hollers to Carl,"We have our crew." Carl hollers back,"Have them go to the safe house clean up the bodies, defused the CIA safe house see if they left behind any intel we can use, did you hear that Arun?"

"I take care of right now boss, when we leave the CIA Safe House, it how you say will be "spick and span" Arun waved to the new crew they all climbed into two trucks and headed back to the house. On the way there they picked up Johnny's body, "Hey boss he begin to stink,"I know we have to pick up all the bodies and bury them, then we have to dis-arm the C4 and search the house."

It took the crew a couple of hours to clean up, Arun was an explosive expert finally the house was cleared for them to enter." Look for any documents they may have left, check the shredder there may be something we can put together, bring everything you find and place it on the kitchen table." The men found a couple of cryptic messages and a basket full of shredded paper that the crew didn't have a chance to destroy.

Arun lays the messages side by side on the table trying to make sense of them,"Dump the shredded paper on the table and start putting them together so we can read what is said."Arun watches as the shreds are placed side by side finally the message began to make sense. It read ,"Will meet with Thai Special Ops at rendezvous tomorrow night."

Arun,"Lets go put all of the paper in that box laying on the floor, hurry, hurry." The men do as told Arun has a huge grin on his face thinking,"I have saved face, Carl will reward me, the CIA knows when and where the arms are to be delivered." They climb into the trucks drive back to the Compound, Arun has the men dismount and take up firing positions around the perimeter of the building, after he is sure the men are well placed, grabs the box and takes off running for the main entrance, he enters the building breathless,"Boss, boss I found correspondence that shows they know about the weapons delivery, come see."

Carl and Henry are in the Great Room having another drink,"What the hell is that racket? tell Arun to keep it down I can't think."Arun walks into the Great Room carrying the box full of Intel,"Boss I found messages left by the CIA, they know about the weapons delivery."

Henry and Carl both jump off the couch as if something had just taken a bite out of their asses,"Put that box on the table let's have a look at it."

He dumps the contents on the table begins to lay out the messages and shredded paper,"Here boss we taped some of the shredded messages and this one reads that they are to meet the Thai military in two days in the south of Thailand." Carl looks at Henry,"How in the hell could they know about the delivery unless, we have a spy in the Compound."Henry posits,"Maybe the Cartel or Insurgents have an mole, it could be anyone we have to be very careful." Carl calls for his encrypted phone, he orders everyone else out of the room,"Henry, do me a favor take this wand check everything in the room for bugs."

Henry sweeps the room, their clothes and the furniture, "Nothing, the room is clean, we'll have to modify our plan for the delivery of the weapons."Finally Carl dials the phone it rings three times and someone on the other end answers,"Code please." Carl answers,"The Chairman will have tea tonight", there is a second of silence,"and what does he have in the tea?" Carl answers,"four lumps","I will connect you to Ling Yun please wait."

"How are you Carl are we on for our meet?"Ling Yun asks. "Yes, the same coordinates as before, we need to talk for a few minutes at the meet there is a matter of great importance we must discuss. It will greatly influence our business dealings in the future." Ling Yun answers,"Understand completely, see you same time and place." Henry,"who in the hell was that?" My contract with the MSS (Chinese Ministry of State Security)he's their man in Cambodia and Thailand, when we meet tonight if there is an imbed he will find him and put a bullet in the back of his head."Carl chuckles. At midnight Carl calls Arun,"Split you'r men up and and take both trucks I want one truck to go west and one to drive east, you have five minutes, move."

"Henry, throw on a disguise and follow me, there is a car waiting in the woods down the road. If they have a spy in the sky hopefully the CIA will follow one of the trucks." They waited till the trucks were on the road they left the Compound walked into the woods and disappeared, the coats they were wearing were manufactured out of new type of material that was designed to hide body heat." The technician controlling the satellite in Virginia hollers,"Son of a bitch they have disappeared, I can't find any trace of them, or the car." His superior calls out,"Leave the satellite overhead, keep the drone circling activate the GPS on the car, if we can't see them at least we can have a good idea where they are going. Henry leans over taps the driver on the shoulder,"Pull over next to that sign and turn off the car, we'll wait here." The wait was short lived, a Mercedes limousine pulls alongside the car, the window is rolled down, the voice in the dark,"Hurry get in the limo before the satellite can get a lock on us." They changed cars, Henry waved to their driver to turn the car around and proceed in the opposite direction.One mile down the road the Mercedes turned into an open garage, the door closed behind them."Ok, people we should be safe from our friends the CIA, this house is designed to misdirect any attempt to penetrate our defenses.Ling Yun embraces Carl and shakes hands with Henry, I will have one of our people from the Gothic Panda set you up with our latest technology, so you will be able to ascertain when they have you in their sights. Come let's eat and you can inform me as to what our problem is."

They all enter a sealed room approximately twenty feet long and twelve feet wide, there is food on the table and a few bottles of Baijiu on the table Ling picks up a bottle and toasts,"gyon bay to our Chinese vodka."

Everyone raises their glass and shouts "gyon bay, gyon bay." Ling starts the conversation,"Alright gentlemen lets get down to business, the weapons are stored in the bunker next door I will have my men load them in a truck while my friend Carl and Henry hash out any perceived problem."

They wait till everyone leaves to load the weapons,"So my friends what is the problem?" Carl,"We think there is an imbed in you'r operation, we have positive proof that the CIA knows about the weapons sale, when and where, the Compound has been checked from top to bottom and we can't find any listening devices."

Ling sits for a few minutes before answering,"Are you sure they aren't using a long range listening device, someone could sit across the street and listen to every word you say.We have a modulator that will scramble the conversation, I'll make sure one of my men gives you the equipment to solve the problem, if that doesn't help just shoot a couple of them."

"Uh, Ling we need a half a million on deposit before we deliver the package" Carl quips. Ling,"The money is in the briefcase under the table" Ling places the case on the table and when he opens it there is a half a million in hundred dollar bills. "Ok we are in, the weapons will be delivered in forty eight hours, warn the Insurgents the CIA and Thai Military are going to try and stop the delivery."

The trucks were loaded Henry and Carl head directly for the coast,"I think we should divide the cache up on four boats just in case we run into trouble.The lead boat will land six miles from the town, then we land another boat two miles south, the third boat two miles further south get the plan, our ETA is 3:am." It was an hour before sunrise the weapons were parked under a makeshift canvas tent to hide the trucks from being observed from a satellite. Carl,"The Insurgents have been made aware that the Thai military and The CIA were waiting in Pattani they are going to set up a diversion to keep the Thai's busy while we unload the weapons and scoot the hell out of there."Henry turns to Carl and asks,"When do you think we should start loading the boats?"

Carl," As soon as it gets dark, we'll beach the boats and unload as soon as we arrive, our customers will be waiting. By four in the morning we should be on our way back to Cambodia." As the boats are being unloaded they heard gun fire,"They must have engaged the Thais, hope they kill a few of those bastards.Oh God!I wish I could have a crack at Marjorie."

Henry just looks at Carl,"Let's get this load off the boat and get the hell out of here, enough already we need to get back to Cambodia, if they interdict the boat we are dog meat." The boat was cleared for the run back to home base there was a slight fog sliding silently across the water, it would make it almost impossible to detect their escape.

CHAPTER TEN

After their initial fire fight with the enemy everything was suddenly quiet. The Major turns looks at Morrison, "What the hell just happened." Morrison answers,

"Why don't you ask your prisoners? I am sure with a little persuasion they would be happy to talk."

The Major calls to his men,"Bring the prisoner with the head wound over here so I can question him."

Two soldiers drag the prisoner over and drop him face down in the dirt, one of the soldiers starts to kick the prisoner in the ribs."I don't want him dead, I said I wanted to question him sit him up against the tree."

The soldiers set him against a tree and back off,"Where are the rest of your comrades? You stinking piece of shit, when I get done with you, your own mother won't recognize you." The prisoner looks at the Major and starts to laugh,"Go screw your self I will never tell you anything, you'r stupid we have what we need to kill all infidels. We will burn your Temples and bring fire upon all non-believers." The Major turns to one of his men,"Hand me the hood and a bucket of water." The Major pulls the hood over the prisoners head and ties it snugly around his neck, he picks up the bucket of water and slowly pours it over the mans face, after the third time the prisoner screams,"Please, please our attack was a ploy to keep you busy while the weapons were unloaded." He spits on the Major, before Charley or Morrison can stop him he pulls his pistol and KAPOW, KAPOW shoots the prisoner between the eyes saying,"You'll never spit on anyone again you piece of shit."

Charley asks Major Kiet,"Let us take the other prisoner and see what intel we can squeeze out of him, he can't do us any good dead. Come on be reasonable, you and your men need to see if they can capture part of the weapons cargo.Our spy in the sky has eyes on two loads of weapons they are only a few clicks from here on a dirt road that parallels the water." Major,"Everyone move we have our honor to protect, he jumps in the lead vehicle Charley I will call you in the morning after the Insurgents are captured."

They all stood there watching as the Thais disappeared into the jungle. Marjorie was the first to break the silence, "Wow, I wouldn't want to get on his bad side, he is one cold blooded bastard." Mike speaks,"This is all about losing face and our Major has made sure that his men know what happens if they make him loose face, as he watches the Major slowly place his pistol in his holster just standing smiling.On the way to capture the weapons the Major calls in air support,"Put two copters in the air there are three trucks loaded with weapons heading north of us, if necessary destroy the enemy, but first try to stop them, we are just a few minutes south of the target." The armored vehicles are driving parallel with the fleeing Insurgents," We should be just ahead of the trucks, turn toward the bay so we can cut them off." When the Thai troopers broke out of the jungle the armored car was just ahead of the first truck, the second armored vehicle was running parallel with the middle truck, the Lieutenant ordered his man on the machine gun to fire,"Trooper stop that truck at all costs."

The gunner opens up with the top mounted machine gun it rips through the cab of the truck cutting the driver and passenger in half. The truck gives a wild lurch and careens into the jungle flipping over on it's side and bursts into flames."That's one truck full of weapons that won't be used by the Insurgents, keep moving if it is loaded with ammo it will blow any minute."

The driver of the armored car speeds up and is advancing on the lead truck. The Lieutenant is watching in the rear view mirror the last truck in the convoy has sped up trying to get past the burning vehicle. Just when it appears the driver will accomplish his mission the burning vehicle explodes into a huge fireball that lights up the night sky. The force of the explosion is so fierce that it knocks the truck sideways and sets the rear canvass on fire, the two occupants flee the truck and run for the jungle. The Lieutenant starts to laugh,"We have an early sunrise and I'll bet those two will have a hell of a time shaking the shit out of their pants."

Up ahead the lead armored car is sitting crossways in the road with the machine gun aimed at the lead ammo truck. Major Kiet stands in the road with his automatic weapon directly at the driver,"Get out of the truck now, or I will gladly send you to your heaven, now move!"

As the men exited the truck, they were ordered to,"Lay face down on the road and put your hands behind your back."

The driver did as he was told, but the other Insurgent pulled up his rifle and as he was about to shoot the Lieutenant in the back, the soldier manning the armored car machine gun saw the flash of the weapon and fired a burst into his body, he fell to the ground and with his last grasp on life pulled the pin from a grenade hooked to his belt. Everything happened in slow motion the gunner on the armored vehicle dropped into the armored car pulling the hatch closed behind him, the Lieutenant dove for cover behind the truck, the Insurgent truck driver with his hands tied behind him stood up running like hell for the woods. There was a loud explosion and then another, the armored vehicle rocked but was undamaged, Lieutenant Aimoads exposed legs received the brunt of the blast the fleeing Insurgent was captured, as he fell into a pig wallow,"Screaming please don't kill me, please don't kill me." The Lieutenant stood up he had superficial burns, "Bring that asshole to me and throw him into the back of the truck. He will have the pig shit cleaned off of him when we get to the Barracks, by the way get those body parts off of my armored car.

Two troopers dismounted from the Vehicle and removed the arm and leg from the hood and some human intestines stuck to the radiator. The Lieutenant said,"We'll clean the rest off at the Motor Pool." He looked at Major Kiet for conformation, Major Kiet shook his head yes. The CIA contingent had witnessed this entire fire fight.

Morrison asks Charley,"Now what, do we follow the Thais or look for Carl and Henry?" He ponders for a second,"I say we follow Major Kiet and see what information can be gleaned from the prisoner. I'm sure our friends are long gone by now they are probably headed for the Compound. We have eyes on the target twenty four hours, when those two are back in town I will know."They followed behind the Armored Vehicles for three hours, when they arrived at the Army Base Major Kiet sent one of his men to greet the group,"Major say you stay in barracks tonight, he will question prisoner late morning.Every one headed for the barracks it was thirty six hours since anyone had slept. The group hit the mattresses, at eleven in the morning there was a rap on the barracks door,"Major say time you people awake, he is going to question the prisoner."

When they were ready to face the world the crew was taken to the base prison,Marjorie looks at the building and quips,"Nice place but I sure as hell wouldn't want to be a guest here." They were ushered into the interrogation room, there sits the truck driver with a hood over his head, pants pulled down around his ankles with battery cables attached to his testicles. Charley lets out a loud,"Oh shit." The Major looks up and smiles,"Relax Charley he will live but I don't know if he will be able to breed when we are done with him."

"Sit down, everyone sit down and watch as we question the prisoner,Morrison whispers to Mike and Marjorie,"We can't be here if the authorities were to be told we were here we could go to jail, Major if you please we must remove ourselves from the interrogation. Our Government will charge us with being involved with torturing a prisoner." Major,"I understand, we have no such rules in Thailand I can use any means necessary to make prisoners confess their crimes."They stepped out of the building and as they were soaking up the tropical sun, Marjorie commented,"I have been dreaming of screwing with Carl's balls, but he wouldn't live through what I have in store for him." All of a sudden there is a scream that echoes from the prison, they can hear the pain career from wall to wall and the sound stops, a man is crying,"I will tell you what ever you want to know, please no more!"Major Kiet opens the prison door smiling,"It's amazing what a shock to the testicles, plus the removal of a few fingernails will do for one's memory." Charley just grimaces,"Major you are one sick son of a bitch, by the way what did you learn?"

Major,"He spilled his guts, we know who the ring leaders are, there was a Buddhist Monk killed and he confirmed my suspicion as to who the killer was. I am moving him and his family to a safe house in the capital, he's on his own from there.Why don't you and your friends stay for a few days"

Charley,"Sorry we have to keep eyes on Carl's Compound in Cambodia. Those two are wanted by our Government on multiple charges, murder, rape, gun and drug running you name it, we have to lure them out of Cambodia so they can be deported back to the states."

Marjorie asks the Major,"Were you able to find out where the weapons were manufactured?"

Major,"The weapons were made in China and Russia. The Chinese in particular have been trying to make inroads for the last few years and the Russians are into white slavery and drugs. They are a hard bunch to get a handle on I will send you a full report when you return to the American Embassy in Bangkok."

The Major calls to his Aide,"Have one of our men take our friends to the airport, they have a plane waiting. See them off safely then report back to me, understand." "Yes sir, please follow me.I will drive you to the airport." When they arrived at the airport there was a private jet waiting for them, Charley,"Ok people we have a lot of work ahead of us when we get to the Embassy in Bangkok." They bypassed security and boarded the plane.

CHAPTER ELEVEN

On the flight to Bangkok Charley's encrypted phone rings he answers it,"Hello, who is this?" There is a slight pause,"Is this Charley?, it's the Ambassador in Bangkok when you land I would like to meet with you tomorrow at the Embassy say four o'clock. There is a problem we need taken care of immediately." Charley answers,"Yes sir I will be there at four o'clock, should I bring the rest of the crew?"

Ambassador,"No, you can read them in later, our friends the Russians are up to their old tricks we need to put them in their place.There will be a limo waiting at the airport I have reservations for your crew at the Bangkok Hotel the rooms have been vetted, so we don't have the same problems as before",the Ambassador answered his question before he asked."He clicked off the phone,"Ok people, we have a new mission when we land in Bangkok, I have to see the Ambassador at four o'clock tomorrow, after the meeting I will read you in. We stay at the Bangkok Hotel, questions?" Morrison asks,"What about Carl and Henry are we going to forget about those two dirt balls?" Charley,"I doubt it they may be involved, I won't know till I meet with the Ambassador tomorrow.It sounds like a problem that has to be taken care of immediately."

The rest of the flight is with out interruption, when they arrive they are picked up and at the hotel, head for their suites on the top floor. Morrison,"Mike and Marjorie wand the place it is supposed to be vetted, but anything is possible with the Russians and Chinese staying here."

Marjorie,"The place seems clean I don't pick up any signals." Mike,"Same here."

Morrison puts his finger to his lips and writes on a piece of paper,"Look under the furniture, check the phone and lights. I would bet this place is bugged."

Marjorie takes the phone apart and sure as hell it is bugged, she climbs on a chair and checks the chandelier one of the bulbs is a camera,"These bastards are like lice, I would sure like to get my hands on one of them and stick this camera up their ass." Charley was checking his suite he had the same problem,"So much for the Suites being vetted, as soon as our people left they re-bugged the damned place." Morrison,"You two go next door and see if Charley can use help." They knocked on the door, Charley opened it,"I need help this place is full of bugs."

Mike lifted the lid to the toilet, he stopped in midair

"I need help, this shit house is boobytrapped.There's a wire leading to it. A phone someplace in the hotel can probably set it off or I bet if the toilet is used there is also a pressure plate under the seat. When the user attempts to stand it will explode." Charley,"Put the lid down and lets get the hell out of here, this hotel is worse except for Nam, somebody wants us gone, and don't care how."

He calls the Embassy,"We need a safe house they must have re-bugged the suites as soon as our people left and to put the topper on it we found a booby trap in the toilet.

They all packed up and left the hotel took a cab to the Embassy. The CIA Chief in residence met them at the door,"Charley somebody is warning us to keep hands off, you and your crew meet me in the conference room, leave your phones, watches, and pens at the desk. When they were all seated an officer entered the room and checked everyone for anything that would send a signal,"Everybody seems to be clean, do you need me to stand by just incase boss?"

"No, we should be ok for now, just stand outside I will call if you are needed."

He walked to a large board on the wall and started the meeting,"There is chatter that the North Koreans and Russians are going to dump one hundred million dollars in fifty and hundred US dollar bills on the market.We have our work cut out for us number one, the compound in Cambodia will be under surveillance twenty four hours a day, number two the bogus money is coming in from Laos through Cambodia we surmised that the North Koreans will try to get it to the states one of two ways, by cargo ship or by plane, number three, drugs and white slavery. The Cambodian government has promised to keep the Thai authorities informed, but they are in bed with the Chinese Government who is pumping millions into the Cambodian economy, hopefully we can interdict the White Slavers and Drug Dealers before they can distribute their cargo throughout the area."

Marjorie is sitting at the bar having a double martini, dirty with three olives. She twirls the swizzle stick slowly watching the olive slide up and down, thinking,"The more I think about it something doesn't click, every time we get close to Henry and Carl they are able to check us.

It's like they know what our plans are."

Morrison sitting next to her asks,"What are you thinking, I can see the wheels turning?"

She slowly sets the swizzle stick in the martini glass, turns around and grins,"We are being set up, every time we try to nail those two scum bags they slip between our fingers, either we have a mole in the organization or somehow the enemy is intercepting our communications."

Morrison thinks for a second,"We are using the latest encryption techniques, according to the home office the CIA is miles ahead of our enemies."

Marjorie,"Bullshit, bullshit, bullshit I wouldn't be surprised if we don't have the Chinese following our every move, they could even have a make believe patriot putting the screws to us.I say we have a leak Christ, we could even be bugged!" Morrison,"Jesus, calm down Marjorie, the entire bar is watching,I say we take a walk and think this out." As they walked out of the bar and stepped on the sidewalk a Chinese business man picks up his briefcase, slowly follows the couple out of the hotel. Chinese business man,"I have them in sight the audio is ninety three percent. Comrade the Agents are walking towards sixth street you will be able to take a perfect picture of them when they turn the corner." Comrade,"Ok, we have everything we need, break off before the CIA Agents spot you, I'll meet you at the lab in the Chinese Embassy where we can put this all together."

Marjorie looks over her shoulder and notices a Chinese Business man talking into his blue tooth, he looks up abruptly turning one eighty crossing the street. He definitely did not want to be recognized. Marjorie grabs Morrisons shoulder, "Did you see that?the son of a bitch was following us, I wonder what that was all about?" Morrison,"Who the hell knows they seem to have eyes on all of us, you are right we have a mole in our organization.The thing is how do we smoke him or her out?"

Screeching of tires,"Hey Morrison you are a dead man" before he can pull his Glock two men tackle him, he hits the pavement hard he spins around the attackers are running down the street."Shit, they are out of range if I shoot I might hit a pedestrian. He looks around Marjorie, is no where to be found. Morrison,"What the hell is going on?" Kidnapper,"Boss said he wants her alive so he can kill her himself."

"She is one crazy bitch, Sap her, put her out of my misery she is driving me nuts." Marjorie screams,"You Goddamned moron get these cuffs off me now or I'll rip your nuts off." The kidnapper holding her down,"Laughs, shut up or I will smash your head in."

Before he can finish the sentence Marjorie rolls over kicking the gun out of his hand, as he reaches backward to grab the gun she bites him square on the balls.

"A..aaaa, let go of me you crazy bitch." She clamps down harder he drops the gun and falls backward with a loud groan, his body starts to tremble as he passes out.

Marjorie grabs the keys and unlocks the cuffs mumbling,"The stupid asshole should know better than cuff me with my hands showing."

The driver is trying to watch the road and see what is happening in the rear of the SUV," Jake, you alright?" Jake doesn't answer he pulls to the side of the road and reaches for his gun,"You are one dead broad, I don't care what Carl wants." He turns to shoot and Marjorie wraps the cuffs around his arm pulling it backward and down, there is a loud snap as the arm is broken at the shoulder."Oh my God, Oh my God, she broke my shoulder." She undocks the rear door rolls her kidnapper out of the car, catches the driver with a kick to the temple knocking him out cold, opens the drivers door,"Tell Carl to kiss my Lilly white ass, the next time I see him, I'm going to cut off his balls and he will be wearing them on his chin."

Marjorie jumps into the drivers seat pulls a wheelie and heads back to town. Morrison calls for help,"We have a situation one of our people has been kidnapped."

Morrison looks up as Marjorie pulls up to the curb,"The two morons that grabbed me are laid out on the road about five miles south."He climbs into the SUV,"Lets go before they get their second wind."Shadows cast by the headlights picked up the two bodies laying in the road."They are still where I left them, what a pair of idiots."

Morrison stops just short of the two. He unholsters his Glock and exits the car, Marjorie is right behind him. She walks over to the driver, kicks him in the ribs,"Come on dick head put your hands on your head and roll over, make any fast moves and I will put a bullet in you, now move." "Jesus Christ, you broke my arm have mercy, I can't rollover."

Marjorie pats the driver down,"Ok stay as you are, Morrison what about the other one is he moving?"

"He's breathing I'm calling for backup we need an ambulance and Thai troops to haul these two back to our home base for questioning." It takes forty five minutes for the ambulance to arrive. The Medics unload stretchers and approach the two men on the road,"Whoa, whoa, I need to see your credentials, where are the Thai Police?"

The Medics reach for their identification.Marjorie,"Stop, put the stretchers on the ground, place your hands on the top of your heads now!,Morrison keep them covered while I search them." She notices the foreword Medic is sweating profusely, the other Medic walks behind his partner whispering,"Get down on your knees, don't move or I will blow your head off." Morrison has taken aim at the forward Medic," Marjorie cuff him and back off so I have a good shot." He motions towards the Ambulance and signs that there appears to be at least two more people in the Ambulance. Marjorie thinks,"Shit we are out numbered and out gunned. Morrison had the cover of the SUV but I'm standing in the line of fire." Morrison slowly opens the car door and grabs a machine gun from the seat, there is a shadowy figure exiting the rear of the Ambulance.

Immediately there is the sound of automatic fire, the front Medic turns pulls a pistol and starts to shoot, Marjorie places two bullets center mass the would be shooter falls over with a gasp blood gurgling from frosty lips stone dead, she dives for the cover of the SUV cracks the second Medic on the head knocking him cold rolls behind the safety of the car just as Morrison fires a volley at the gunman.

"God damn it we need backup, we either abandon the prisoners and get the fuck out of here or we're dead. There must be half a dozen hostiles in that truck, where in the hell are the Thai troops." Marjorie,"Who did you call because he must be one of them, probably the mole we were

trying to find."Morrison signs to Marjorie to get in the car he, slides over and grabs the wheel, starts the engine showering the advancing hostiles with gravel, she gunned the engine.They disappear in the distance. Marjorie,"Do you think they will pursue us?" Morrison,"After they clean up the mess I would guarantee it, get on the encrypted phone and call the safe house we need a copter to pick us up ASAP!"

Chapter Twelve

They watched as the gun ship landed on the blacktop, Pilot,"Hurry up we spotted car lights about twenty minutes away I think you two have pissed off every Thai within fifty miles" the pilot hollered.

As the copter glided over the trees there was the sound of gunfire, "We just made it, a couple of minutes and we would have been hamburger." Morrison started to laugh,"Our next stop is Cambodia we take out Carl and Henry, Charley is in league with a War Lord to infiltrate the compound, he has a blood feud with Carl apparently he raped one of his cousins and wants revenge."

Meanwhile at the Drug Compound,Carl pours two glasses of wine handing one to Henry,"Here's to the end of those two, I just hope their deaths were slow and painful."

They snort a few lines strip down for the orgy, it is two in the morning, the guards are half drunk or sleeping. A block away three trucks park the occupants silently dismount dressed in black, faces covered with hoods. The tribesmen slip through the darkness their weapons wrapped to muffle the noise, grappling hooks are attached to the roof, C4 is placed on the rear and front doors the leader gives the signal and all hell breaks loose. The entrances and the roof are simultaneously breeched, the explosions rock the Drug Compound.Henry jumps up trying to get his pants on Carl rolls off the bed falling like a piece of dirt on the floor, leaving Carls two naked beauties running for the door. "Jesus Christ, what the hell is happening?"

Carl screams,"We're being attacked it's that Frigging War Lord he's still pissed that I raped his cousin and wouldn't pay zina (the bride price) he promised to castrate me."

Henry,"Run for the tunnel let's get the hell out of here." The sound of gunfire was getting closer, the hall was covered in blood from the rugs to half way up the walls.

Men were trying to surrender,"Please! we give up don't shoot." There was the sound of gunfire then silence. Carl and Henry opened the false door in the bedroom wall, ran like they were on fire down the tunnel that led across the street and exited in the rear of an abandoned building.

Henry,"Now what we need is transportation out of here." Carl,"I have a truck parked in the alley." They pulled out onto the street, the flashes of gunfire could be seen through the Compound windows as they drove away. After driving two hours Carl slowed down and took stock of what had just happened."I'll bet the CIA was behind this attack." That's what we get for letting our guard down, Charley knew about the blood money he set that Crazy Towel head on us. I can feel it in my bones ,there's the plane it will take us to a Chinese base in Laos, we will be able to set up our operation and run weapons from there".

The prop on the plane sputtered to life after a short run the plane was airborne, three hours later the the sun was setting in the west as they approached the Laos airstrip the green lush jungle opened up it's canopy to the landing strip, the roar of the engines echoed through the jungle causing the monkeys to scream their annoyance and the birds to take flight.

"We'll be on the ground in a couple of minutes, I will have to convince our Comrade Chin that the attack on the Compound is a minor setback" Carl cautioned Henry to let him do the talking. They deplaned, climbed into a waiting truck flanked by armed guards,"Henry whispers to Carl,"What the Hades is going on are we prisoners or what?" Carl,"I'm sure Comrade Chin is pissed the surprise attack on our compound in Cambodia caused the loss of ten million worth of drugs. His superiors I am sure are barking up his ass and he wants to take it out on us."The truck stopped in front of a large mansion, one of the guards climbed out of the truck motioning for Carl and Henry to follow."Well here goes we'll have to kiss Chin's butt, I have a contact in Vietnam that can deliver all the weapons we will need to supply the insurgents in the south plus heroin by the ton, the Vietnamese don't trust the Chinese government. They want too much control."

They entered Chin's office he was sitting at his desk and ignored them letting the pair stand wondering what he was up to finally looked up," Sit down and keep quiet I should have the two of you shot. Carl that cock of yours is going to be the death of you, enough of this shit lets get down to business." Chin rolls a map out on his desk,"There is an arms shipment destined for Vietnam on the Mekong River that will be close to Laos, Colonel Wei will take charge of the shipment and you two will deliver it to the "AA" in Indonesia the Government is having a small uprising in the villages and my government wishes to keep their armed forces occupied as a warning that our Indoctrination Camps controlling the Uyghur's is a Chinese internal affair."

Henry,"How in the hell are we to deliver the weapons, we don't have a clue who this "AA" is or why they are fighting." Colonel Wei smiles,"I will educate both of you, because if the weapons are not delivered Comrade Chin has ordered me to turn you over to the Military or even better bury the pair of you in the sand and let the bugs eat you alive, Ha,Ha,Ha!!,I make joke yes?"

Carl,"I have a feeling we are being set up to take a fall, Comrade Chin what can we do to fix the problem?"

Chin,"I have put up with your screwing things up for the last time I have lost face, all you assholes do is screw around and make enemies this time there will be no mistakes, Colonel escort them to the barge."Carl and Henry are escorted out of Chin's office and loaded into an armored vehicle surrounded by armed guards."I think your friend Chin is pissed off and plans to make an example of us" Henry wisecracks.

Carl,"Somehow we have to slip off that barge before it docks or we will be fish bait." After about an hour the truck comes to a stop. Soldier,"Alright put those two in the aft cabin, chain the door, I'll take care of them when we are almost to the rendezvous." Henry surveys the interior of the cabin, there are bars on the windows and the cabin door is metal clad, he starts to look for a weakness by pulling on the wood slats used to enclose the cabin.

Chapter Twelve

Henry sees that the wood under the window appears to be rotten puts his foot against the wall pulls with all his strength, it crumbles in his hands. Henry,"Carl give me a hand we should be able to open a hole big enough to get the hell out of here." They both pulled together the wood under the window gave way with a loud crunch, Carl and Henry held their breath no one on deck seemed to hear.

"Let's go brother before they decide to off us." Both men wiggle through the hole sliding themselves quietly into the Mekong River. They swim to shore, hid in the jungle till the barge sailed out of sight,"That barge was heading south not north the story we were given was pure bullshit.I'll bet Chin is selling the arms to the pirates and pocketing the money." Carl,"There is a village up the road maybe we can find someone to ferry us across to the other side I have contacts in Vietnam, we can clean up and maybe get revenge on Comrade Chin that slant eyed thief is going to try to take over our territory."

When they entering the village Carl asked a villager,"Who is the village spokesman or head man, can we speak to him?" The woman took them to a hut along the river she pulled back a curtain,"Please sit the chief will be here shortly." After a few minutes he entered," What can I do for you gentlemen?" Carl,"Is their anyone in the village that can ferry us across to the other side? they will be well paid." "My son has a small boat with a motor he can do as you wish, the price is one hundred American paid up front." Carl opens his wallet and hands the Head man a credit card, Head Man,"Mother bring me the credit card terminal." She sets it on the table inserts Carl's card,"Ten bucks extra for the charge." Hands the card back to Carl." Head Man,"I deal with tourists all the time have to keep up with the times."

Carl and Henry look at each other and start laughing,"I wondered why you spoke perfect english." Head Man,"I can tell you two are on the run, I'll get you across the river and my contacts will take you to Hanoi from there you are on your own." He snapped his fingers and four armed villagers entered the hut,"Escort these two men across the river and tell Bao to take them to Hanoi."

Carl and Henry climbed into the boat followed by their guards,"You two sit in the front of the boat and don't move till we reach the shore." An hour later the boat was tied to the dock."Out,Out!Take the path to the left Bao's hut is about a mile he is waiting for you." They exited the boat started walking down a rut in the jungle.Carl,"I think we should try to talk our friend Bao to take us to Saigon better known today as Ho Chi Minh City, I'm sure we can find a drug dealer to supply us with a new stash."

Henry spots a light in the darkness,"That must be the hut maybe old Bao can be bribed?" They parted the curtains at the doorway, an old woman sat at a handmade bamboo table, the oil lamp on the table lit the inside of the hut casting eyrie shadows against the interior walls covered in moss.In the corner Henry spied children sleeping on a built up wooden bed."We are looking for Bao is he available?"The old woman cackled,"My son will be back later you sit please." Carl,"I hear a truck coming maybe it's our boy." They watched as the truck parked the driver left the engine running, opened the drivers door and hollered,"Are you my pick up going to Hanoi?" Carl answered,"We changed out minds we want to go to Saigon will pay you what ever the extra charge is."

The driver,"No can do my orders are to take you to Hanoi." "I will pay you another one hundred dollars American." "No can do Hanoi!" Carl,"Ok,Ok, Hanoi it is, come on Henry let's get going." Carl looks at Henry putting his finger to his lips signing to keep silent, they climb into the truck the driver backs the truck around drives down the road throwing dirt and stones, dust so thick the road was almost engulfed in the storm of debris that is stirred up."Henry screams,"Slow down you asshole before you get us killed!!" The driver ignores Henry,"He pulls out his pistol and placed it against the drivers temple,"I said stop you son of a bitch or I'll blow your dumb brains out."

Looking in the mirror the driver seeing the gun at his temple, jammed on the breaks throwing Carl and Henry against the dashboard,"You God damned idiot get out of the truck before I frigging kill you." Henry reaches over opens the drivers door kicking the driver into the road.

He slides into the drivers seat turns the key,"Lets get the hell out of here." Looking in the rearview mirror watches as the driver stands up and runs into the jungle.

Carl sets the GPS on the dashboard,"Head straight south we were near Hue it will take us all night to make Ho Chi Minh City. About half way to Ho Chi Minh Henry pulled over,"Carl you take over I need a break, we should be in the city by about noon."Carl drove till they were in the inner city.

Henry asks,"Where in the hell are we?" Carl,"Keep your shirt on only a few more blocks and we'll be there, this is the place Apocalypse Now Bar they have a bundle for us."

There were about a dozen hookers plying their trade in front of the bar. Hookers,"Hey boys looking for a good time? I can do what ever you want. Carl,"Look sweetheart I don't have time right now we are looking for Big Joe the owner." Hooker,"He's inside checking the nights take." When they tried to enter the Apocalypse the bouncer stepped up stopping them from entering."Ten dollars each." Henry,"Look moron we have an appointment with your boss so step aside and let us in."

The bouncer was about six feet two and built like a bull, reached out to grab Henry by the throat,"You shut the fuck up white boy." Henry as quick as a snake reaches down and grabs the bouncer by the testicles and twists, the bouncer goes down on his knees there's a flash of a sap as it smashes the Bouncers head, blood gushes like a fountain splattering Henry's coat."You slimy bastard look what you did." He puts his foot in the bouncers chest and pushes him violently causing him to fall over backwards, he lay on the steps groaning.

Carl laughs,"Come on Henry leave the poor SMUCK we have business to take care of." They open the bar doors and walk into bedlam, there is a band playing country music and naked strippers selling drinks and sexual favors. "Henry keep your dick back in your pants, looks like the office is over there we can party after we pick up the drugs."

Carl stopped at the office door and knocked, the door opened automatically there was Big Joe sitting behind his desk, "Gentlemen come in I have been expecting you." He handed Carl the money and a paper with the address,"Be there at eight tomorrow morning and pick up the stuff, by the way Carl can you keep that Troll from hurting any of my boys on the way out." Henry flares,"Screw you asshole I'll give you a Troll." Carl,"Let's go Henry he's busting your balls."

Carl laughs. They walk through the insanity of the bar and step out into a fog so thick the birds are grounded."I want to be at the pickup tonight don't trust anyone in this business, I want to make sure we aren't being scammed." Henry,"We don't have any fire power." Carl,"I know a GI that went native in town I will guarantee he has any thing we need for sale." When they arrived at the store it was totally dark."Doesn't look like anybody's home."Carl climbs out of the car and bangs on the door, BANG, BANG," Come on Killer get your butt out of bed."

The lights on the second floor turn on the second floor window slides open they can see the light shining on a shotgun peeking out of the window. Henry,"Holy shit he's going to blow us away."

Carl,"Killer put the goddamned piece away it's Carl we need to do business." The shotgun disappears a crazy looking man with long unkept hair and a scraggly beard sticks his head out of the open window,"Carl it is you? I heard some War Lord has your head hanging on his wall in revenge for screwing one of his relatives." Carl,"You can't believe those asshole rumors, you know that is a bunch of bullshit, take my word for it."

Killer,"I'll be right down I just brought in a whole boatload of new weapons Tre-Fire, Fire sticks, Ooze, Choppers, how about vests I have Ballistic Level II vests you name it I have it." He opened the shop door. Killer,"Come in Carl I missed your sorry ass, he took them to the rear of the store opened a locked room inside was a terrorists dream, every weapon known to man and then some."Take your pick gentlemen,I can order in anything you want."

Chapter Thirteen

Henry marveled at the array of weapons,"A couple of Ballistic Vests, Choppers and a crate of grenades, OH YEA, two Glocks that should do us."Carl shook his head in agreement.

Killer,"That will be sixty nine hundred dollars American." Carl,"Killer, Jesus I didn't want to buy the Frigging factory, can't you give us a break?" Killer,"Carl, Carl that's the price there's nothing I can do, take it or leave it." Carl,"Henry load the hardware in the car I will pay for the weapons, we need to screw." They drive to the warehouse where they are supposed to pick up the stash and park across the street in the shadows where there is a perfect view of the meet.

"It's four in the morning and I would bet that the boys doing the handoff are already set up inside just waiting for us,"Carl says.Suddenly, a blinding light spreads over the front of the warehouse as one of the gang steps outside to look around, they watch as he walks around the building making sure the coast is clear. They could hear him calling to his men. Sammy,"Before they arrive bring out the machine gun and set it up in the tall grass, Marty park your ass in the back of the truck and Bao take the other side of the building that way we will have them in a cross fire, they will never know what hit them."Henry looks at Carl,"What do we do now? There's no way we can take them all out without getting our butts shot up."

Carl just smiles and picks up the sniper rifle attaching a silencer."It's still dark I can take out at least two of them before they realize what is happening, you kill the one in the truck. From what I observed there are four more in the building after we take out these three we make a lot of noise to draw the others out. I will pick them off as they charge out the door." Henry crouched low like a cobra slithering silently through the jungle, he never made a sound when he was behind the machine gunner there was a sudden flash of moonlight as the knife plunged into the half asleep form Henry jerked the head backwards covering his mouth, he slumped dead over the machine gun without a sound his backbone severed drooling a frost of blood from his lips.

Henry,"Thats one down two to go." He waved to signal Carl that the machine gunner was dead to take out the Hood on the other side of the building. Carl slowly raised the rifle placed the scope on the forehead of his victim, slowly squeezed the trigger and watched as the bullet penetrated his forehead blowing out the back of his skull causing his brains to exploded turning it into a mass of flesh and an inferno of blood and bone. "WOW, his own mother won't recognize that poor bastard", Carl exclaimed.

While Henry was crawling toward the truck the gunman looked up calling for the rest of the crew,"Hey whats going on? you guys are awfully quiet." That was the last sound he would ever make as Henry with the precision of a Ninja played a knife in his heart, eyes wide he did a dance of death as his arms were flailing in a final twist before he fell out of the truck bed with a thud.Henry climbing into the truck bed picked up the machine-gun at the same time waving to Carl that it was a go.Carl hollered for the gang inside of the building to get the hell out side,"HEY MORONS"

,Get out here so I can blow you away" he screams,"I'm talking to you in the warehouse."The warehouse door flies open the crew comes out firing wildly, bullets spraying the trees, the truck you name it. Carl had anticipated this and had moved to the far right of the doorway so the crew were perfect targets outlined by the interior light in the building.

He center shot the first form dead in the chest as the body fell the second shot took the next in line in the temple. The last two ducked back inside slamming the door. Henry raised up firing through the wall where he thought the fleeing gang would be standing, he waited for a second, bolted out of the truck and kicked the door open there were two bodies kissing the concrete, eyes staring into nothingness. Henry calls to Carl,"They are all dead let's grab the stuff and screw I am sure with all this shooting we probably woke the entire neighborhood."

Chapter Fourteen

Marjorie asks,"Have they found Carl and Henry yet?" Jack,"No they are still looking, the driver was found along the side of the road in Vietnam with a concussion and all our contact was able to get out of him was the word "con khi" over and over which means monkey in Vietnamese. It makes no sense." Marjorie,"I will give it to those two they are as slippery as eels, didn't the woman in Thailand describe Henry as a "ling" which means monkey in Thai. They must have traveled south to HO Chi Minh City, I'll bet Henry attacked the driver and forced him out of the truck."

Jack,"My contacts in Ho Chi Minh should be able to get a fix on those two maybe even hold them till we can get custody.Wait,I have info coming in on my secure line." (Code Red, Code Red,The suspects have gone to ground cannot find, believe to have ambushed Local Drug Lord and escaped with millions of dollars in drugs. The entire area is up in arms recommend you stay away till things cool off.)

Marjorie,"That has to be Carl and Henry, they leave death and destruction everywhere they go.I will bet they are taking a jungle road in order to bypass the border guards, their final destination is Cambodia."

Jack opens his computer and sends a coded message,(need drone immediately to survey Laotian southern border, suspects expected to cross in near future.) Answer,(will have the Scan Eagle in air by noon today, will let you know when we spot the target.) "All we can do is wait, just hope the Laotian Government doesn't spot our drone or they will be pissed, I think maybe I should call the local General and advises him of the situation."

He dials General Suvon of the Laotian Military, phone rings three times,"Hello this Southern District Peoples Army how may I help?" Jack,"I need to speak to General Suvon please tell him this is Code Blue 777."There is a silence on the other end of the line,General Suvon answers,"Who is this?" "I am an attache from the American Embassy we are pursuing two fugitives attempting to escape from Vietnam into Laos, my government has a drone in Laotian air space tracking them." The General replied,"You have one hour to confirm and then I will consider it a hostile intrusion of Laotian air space and have your drone destroyed." Marjorie heard the phone slammed down,"Jesus, he sounded pissed." Jack just smiled,"He had to cover his ass I am sure one of his subordinates was listening in, He will file a complaint with our embassy in Thailand and Vietnam. So don't be surprised if we receive a message wanting to know what the hell are we are doing stirring up the natives. Hold on we are receiving a confirmation on the location of the Van.,(found van abandoned approximately thirty clicks inside Laotian border, appears to be abandoned, no hits on thermal imagining hostiles have escaped), Jack,"Those two have evaded us again, I'll be a son of a bitch,"Marjorie please call and have them pull the drone back to the Cambodian border before General Suvon has a stroke."

Marjorie picks up the phone contacts the CIA base in Cambodia,"Abort the mission and return the Scan Eagle to origination, we have info that Mobile Surface to Air Units are in the area. (Understand mission is aborted will be clear of Laotian airspace in one hour).

She hangs up,"Jack I need a break, I'm going down to the hotel bar and have a couple of drinks you want to come?" "Na,I have paper work to complete have a ball."

Marjorie exits the elevator and walks to the lounge it's almost empty just a couple of drunks sitting at the bar. She plants her self at the end as far as possible from the other occupants,"Barkeep, pour me a double shot of Scotch." A bearded customer sitting at the other end tells the bartender,"Give that beautiful lady a drink on me." Marjorie,"That's alright I'm good, this one will do me."

The customer stood exclaiming,"My money no good you bitch I offered you a drink." He was over six foot two and built like a tank. She immediately recognized him as one of the actors she had seen drinking with the Russians,"Thinking this is a set up, these bastards have been waiting to catch one of us alone." She reached for her weapon came up empty,

"Son of a Bitch!I left it in the room." All she could see was this hulk with a look that wanted to kill, he pulled a eight inch knife out of his belt, raised it for the kill and started across the room. Marjorie without thinking threw her drink at his head, picked up the bar stool to hold him off.It didn't slow him down he knocked the stool aside she was thrown against the wall thinking,"What a shitty way to go." There was a gunshot and the animal screamed as his hand exploded he screamed in pain "A..A..A.A,GOD,I kill you,I kill you as he went down on his knees and fell forward his face crashing into the tile floor breaking his nose, squirting blood in all directions.

She turned to see Johnny one of the CIA agents holding a gun,"The rest of you pricks back off, the first one to move gets the next bullet between the eyes, Marjorie get behind me." Johnny pulled a second automatic from his belt and handed it to her. "Keep them here while I call the Thai Police and an ambulance." The Thai Police were already coming through the hotel doors,"Drop your weapons or we shoot." She slowly placed the weapon on the floor and standing up placing her hands on the top of her head.

Johnny lowered his weapon and placed it in his shoulder holster, with his hands up approached the Thai Police,"I am with the US Embassy in Bangkok if you will allow me to show you my credentials."the officer shook his head yes.

Johnny,"This woman is under my protection, she was sitting minding her own business and this ape charged her I shot him in the hand to stop his brutal attack on her, as you can see he is still alive. I would greatly appreciate it if you would keep him in jail till morning, when I can interrogate him." Marjorie,"Wait a minute I have one thing to do before you arrest him." The Police Sergeant,"As you wish Madam." She walked around the prone, groaning figure and kicked him in the balls, there was a scream of pain and then silence. "I think he fainted, would love to interrogate him in the morning, I will give you three to one odds he would beg to talk by the time I finished with this son of a bitch." Marjorie and Johnny watched as they dragged him off to the Paddy

Wagon,"We are all under surveillance I told Morrison and George the Russians and Chinese are colluding and the American contingent is to be eliminated one way or the other." Majorie told Johnny,"I can feel it we are being set up."

They were escorted outside by the Thai Police,"You want me to guard you while you proceed to the American Embassy?" Johnny,"No, thats ok we'll take a company car we have had two of our people watching our vehicles to make sure they aren't boobytrapped or bugged, thanks anyway."

Marjorie's phone rang,"Who in the hell is calling me at this hour, hello who is this?, the person on the other end replied,"Susan Alcott your daughter's guardian there is a problem your daughter is in jail and I am afraid only you can resolve the problem."

Chapter Fifteen

"Marjorie,"What is the problem?" Susan Alcott,"She is implicated in a double homicide, a wealthy couple has been brutally murdered and your daughter Sara's "DNA" and finger prints have been recovered at the scene, she is being held without bail."

"Marjorie just looked at the phone in stunned silence,"Give me a couple of hours and I will call you back."Shit,Shit,Shit, Johnny we have to get back to the Embassy I have to talk to Charley and Jack, my daughter is in deep shit I'm going to have to return to the states to bail my daughter out of jail." Marjorie ride to the Embassy was in complete silence, Marjorie thinking,"What in the hell has my daughter got herself into?" Johnny,"We're here, Charley can you get me out on a CIA flight tonight?" Johnny,"A flight leaves at eleven thirty for DC.I'll call the airport and make sure there's a seat for you"."Ok! Thanks greatly appreciated I'll pack my bag, be down in a couple of minutes."

She climbed into the waiting car Johnny drove her to the airport. Sat in the jump seat as the plane taxied for takeoff, she was trying to wrap her head around the scenario of her daughter killing two people,"What in the hell was my daughter doing to get herself in such a mess. Why wasn't Susan Alcott keeping an eye on her daughter? something definitely is not right."

Twenty hours later the sound of the wheels touching the landing strip woke her up, she straightened her clothes, pulled her blond hair into a bun, put on lipstick and checked herself out in the compact mirror,"I guess that will do for now." When she deplaned the pilot pointed to the sedan sitting next to the hanger,"That's for your use Charley said as long as you need it here's a gas card."

When she arrived at the condo Susan was standing at front of the building waiting for her, Marjorie exited the sedan, asking, "Does she have a Lawyer?" Susan, "No I thought you would want to call someone you are friends with." Marjorie, "I'll call Dominic Maretto he's one hell of a good criminal lawyer, he got the FBI off of my back, let's go upstairs so I can make a few phone calls."

Marjorie looked up Dominic's home phone number and dialed, it was late evening but what the hell, the phone rang twice and a young woman picked up, "Hello". "Is this Dominic Maretto's phone?, short silence, "Yes it is and who is calling?". "Tell Dominic it's Marjorie I need his help can you put him on the phone?" Girlfriend, "I'll see if he's available." She put her hand over the mouthpiece, "He never could stay away from those young things, one of these days he's going to get into a real bind."

"Hello, Dominic here who in the hell is this, It's your old client Marjorie I need a favor my daughter is in jail for a double murder, would appreciate it if you could get her out on bail." Dominic, "Your not talking about that yuppy couple up town that were murdered a couple days ago. That's some juicy shit, they were into all kinds of sweet, kinky sex, so your daughter was involved? hell yes I will definitely take the case, I will meet you downtown at the police station in two hours, in the meantime I will talk to the District Attorney to see what evidence she has against your daughter." Two hours later they meet at the Police Station. Dominic, "Talked to the DA she says the case is air tight I think she's blowing smoke, this Natalie Simpson is known for trying to bullshit the defense." Marjorie, "So where do we go from here?" Dominic, "I get a copy of the police report and we sit down with Sara to hear her side of the story." The phone rang the lawyer Dominic Maretto answered, when he hung up said Marjorie," We will be able to meet with Sara at eight tomorrow morning, after the interview I will see if I can get her bail." Seven the next morning Marjorie was up full of piss and vinegar she called Susan Alcott, who picked up on the first ring," Susan, explain to me how my daughter was allowed to become involved with the murdered couple, from what I can ascertain they were known to be swingers and dealt in drugs"… silence… Susan, "I thought that the stories were a fabrication, I couldn't find any proof of the accusations so I allowed Sara to visit with their daughter Agnes." Marjorie, "If Sara was visiting Agnes where is she?"

Susan Alcott,"When the police arrived Sara was the only other person in the house, according to the Police she was found unconscious, holding the murder weapon and covered in blood.

Her friend Agnes was no where to be found."

Marjorie,"She still among the missing?" Susan,"Yes, maybe she was kidnapped."

Marjorie let the conversation die out thinking,"She is definitely hiding something, I will call my handler and have him see if Susan is somehow involved in this murder, we have been friends for years but now my own blood is involved in a double murder and trying to get information from Susan is like pulling teeth,"Susan I will see you at the jail." Marjorie stood on the steps waiting for Maretto and Susan Alcott, she watched as Maretto drove up in his Jag, he was dressed to the nines as usual. "Marjorie nice to see you, it's a shame about your daughter I had no idea she ran in such questionable company." Marjorie,"Keep your wise ass remarks to your self Dominic, have you talked to Susan today? she was supposed to be here at eight." Maretto,"No, haven't had any communication with her since yesterday" alright let us get this over with." They walked into the Police Station. "We're here to talk to Sara Swift."

The Sergeant called the Detective in charge," Detective Smith,Marjorie Swift and her lawyer are here they're waiting at the desk." Detective Smith,"Send them to the interrogation room, I'll see them there." Marjorie and Maretto were escorted to the holding room, Detective Smith stood there holding the door open,"She's waiting for you." Maretto, "This is privileged so turn off the bugs in the room."

Smith retorts,"Come on Dominic we don't bug Lawyer Client meetings." Dominic as he slams the door answers,"Yea, and I'm friends with the Pope." Sara runs into her mother's arms, "Mommy, mommy I didn't do it" tears running down her cheeks. Marjorie,"Just calm down and tell us exactly what happened." Dominic,"Have they interrogated you without having an adult present?" She was silent for a minute,"Yes they have, that Detective who let you in he has talked to me three times and a female officer asked me questions, they tried to get me to admit I killed Agnes' parents, I said I was drugged and don't remember anything." Dominic,"If they attempt to question you again tell them you want your lawyer present don't believe anything they tell you, do you understand

Sara?" Shaking her head yes, wiped tears from her eyes, answers,"Yes sir." Maretto,"Alright now in your own words tell us what you remember start from he beginning."

("It was about seven Friday night", the phone rang and Miss Alcott answered, she said that we would be delighted to come to a party at their house and eight thirty would be fine and hung up.I asked her who had called, she said it was one of my classmates Agnes, I told her I was tired and had never met this Agnes preferred to stay home she insisted, so I gave in and went with her, she seemed nervous on the drive over. When we arrived she let me out, said

"I'll park the car you go in." The front door was open there was a mean looking man standing in the entranceway, he handed me a soda saying Agnes would be right down, while I was sitting there felt a small prick to the back of my neck and that's all I remember till I woke up with a knife in my hand all covered in blood."

CHAPTER SIXTEEN

Dominic and Marjorie just looked at each other, Marjorie,"Where in the hell is Susan Alcott, where is this Agnes, who was the dude that answered the door? this was a deliberate set up to have my daughter framed for murder."

Dominic picked up the Police report and handed it to Marjorie,"If this was a set up, whoever did it thought of everything this report states #1, this couple didn't have any children, #2, Sara's DNA is all over the house,#3, she had sex with the husband and #4, Susan Alcott claims Sara took the car without permission and she had no idea where she was." Marjorie picked up her phone and dialed Susan, "This is not a working number,"What the hell is going on she has been watching Sara for ten years, since she was six years old."

Dominic,"There is a hearing tomorrow morning, I know the judge. Hopefully she will grant bail.We need to get her the hell out of there." Marjorie hands Sara a clean set of clothes,"This is for tomorrow in court you must look all prim and proper" she hugged her daughter,"I'll see you tomorrow." When she arrived at the condo there was a police car sitting at the curb she passed the Police car and as she was about to enter the building the Patrolman exited the car,"Are you Marjorie Swift?"."Yes I am, what can I do for you officer?" we have bad news a Susan Alcott was killed tonight in a hit and run accident, her address was the same as your condo.Do you know her?"

Marjorie backed up and sat down on the building steps,"What did you say? she was a very good friend of the family.

Where did this happen?" Police Officer,"About two blocks from here an hour ago, we would appreciate it if you could come to the morgue and identify the body." Marjorie was visibly shaken,"Jesus have Mercy what is going on?" I am going to have the Secret Service look into the murdered couple they were into something and were murdered for it my daughter was framed for the murders" can you take me to the morgue I don't think I am in any shape to drive?"

"No problem sweetheart, your time is my time." After Marjorie identified Susan she called her contact at the Secret Service,"There is something going on double murder, a hit and run, my daughter framed for two murders and my being pulled off the Thailand case." Agent,"Ok, send me the names of the murdered couple, their background and the woman killed in the hit and run. I'll see if they knew each other, give me a couple of days to put things together."

Marjorie shut off her phone,"Take me back to my condo I have work to do."At the condo the kitchen table was covered with pictures, notes plastered on the wall Marjorie worked on the puzzle till early morning, a ringing phone woke her,"God, I fell asleep. Shit the bail hearing is in two hours, she stripped naked and climbed into a steaming shower the water relaxed her firm body the stream of water reminded her she hadn't made love in quite awhile,"Lord,Lord I need a man, this undercover shit sure has ruined my sex life." The Judge refused to set bail, the District Attorney was adamant that she refuse bail because of the heinous way the murders were committed.Sara was taken away crying,"Mama, mama help me I'm innocent" still asking for her mother as they took her away.

Marjorie's phone rang,"Hello, this is Sammy I understand you wanted us to do a profile on the Jeffersons and If there was a link to Susan Alcott, do you have a few minutes?" She looked at the phone,"All the time in the world." Sammy,"The Jeffersons were into money laundering, drugs and sex parties, your friend Alcott was a frequent guest at their sex parties, she also liked to snort a few lines of coke.I think somebody got to Susan and threatened to expose her if she didn't do as they asked. Then they murdered her because she was a witness. I believe we were getting too close to the truth, we have been investigating the Jeffersons for a long time trying to get a handle on money laundering and drugs." Marjorie took a deep breath,"So this is what it is all about I smell Carl and Henry, who's next Morrison maybe Charley this is a con, these bastards are all in this together.Do you have pictures of people who were at the sex parties

I want to see if I recognize anyone." Sammy,"the scuttlebutt is that the Jeffersons were skimming off the top when they laundered money for the mob this is what happens when people get greedy. We traced the Made Man who controls the deliveries his name is Carl located in LA, he disappeared about a year ago."

Marjorie,"This son of a bitch set my daughter up, they must be planning to return to the states and are cleaning the slate of anybody they suspect can't be trusted.Carl hates my guts and would do anything to get even with me."

Johnny lays pictures on the desk,"We have had these people under surveillance for two years, we know all the actors and what part they play in the game."

Marjorie perused the photos on the desk she recognized three of the faces a man and two women. The one woman was her daughter's guardian Susan Alcott the other one also looked familiar,"I know this woman she was friends with Susan, her name was Francis don't know her last name and the older man with the gray beard was a retired judge his name was Jonathan Grey, yes that's it Jonathan Grey.

Your telling me he was part of this sex ring, butter wouldn't melt in his mouth."

Detective Sammy,"We are questioning everyone separately trying to piece together exactly what transpired before and after the murders." Marjorie,"Do you really believe my daughter killed that couple?" Sammy,"I don't, I think she was set up, if what you say is true Carl wanted to get revenge for what you did to him he figured the best way was to frame your daughter for murder."

Chapter Seventeen

Two years prior, Derek Watsen was having a drink at an upscale bar when the tall blond walked in sits down next to him, he looked her up and down,"Can I buy you a drink you look thirsty? you sure smell good what say we have a matinee." She threw her hair back,"You are a rude son of a bitch what do I look like a whore?" Derek,"Yea, but a high class whore if I might say so. Why don't we go to my place and spend the afternoon?"

Sam,"My rate is $1,000.00 an hour up front." Derek just smiled,"No problem, what did you say your name was?"

"I didn't but it's Sam just Sam, you have any coke I need a couple of lines then I can do anything you want and then some."

They finished their drinks, Derek had the valet bring his Jag, Sam climbed into the passenger seat with her legs spread and skirt up far enough for the world to see her shaved cunnus,"Like what you see there Derek I can do marvelous things with this little crack honey, you will scream for more when I am done with you."

Derek was in a lather,"Holy shit This is too good to be true."This wasn't' his first rodeo but it looked like it might be his best.He pulled into his condo flipped the Jag keys to the Door Man,"George could you please park my car." The Door Man watched as Derek strolled into the high- rise arm in arm with a tall blond with her skirt so short there was no question that she wasn't wearing any underpants. George,"God what a walk! a man could leave home for her." He smiled and turned opening the door for the next tenant. On the ride up in the elevator she wrapped her sensuous body around his and by the time the elevator doors opened he was totally under her spell,"Come on lover I will screw you till you scream for mercy" entering the condo Derek pulled a bag of coke and made a couple of lines, pulled out two straws they snorted in unison.

They started to take off their clothes leaving a trail behind them as they crashed on the bed in a naked embrace she straddled him started to rotate on his erection Derek went spastic climaxing in minutes."How in the hell did you do that? absolutely fantastic sex tonight."

Tomorrow I am going to the Casino it would make my business associates envious to see someone like you as my escort, what do you say?" Sam,"As long as you can pay my fee."

Derek,"No problem." Sam,"By the way what do you do for a living?"

Derek,"I trade bearer bonds around the world It lets me make a very good living and I can do whatever I wish, got rid of my wife a couple of years ago, no kids free as a bird." Sam,"You don't say I have some friends I can introduce you to they may have an interesting proposition for you" Derek,"If it means more shekels in my pocket I'm all in"Derek commented.

When they were dressed, Derek locked the condo door and the couple headed for the elevator, on the way down he called the Concierge,"Harold bring my sports car around and make sure it is gassed up"."Sure boss give me a couple of minutes."

When they reached the street the valet opened the door for the lady bowing, Derek tipped the Concierge and valet twenty dollars each."See you in the morning, laughing, don't wait up."

When they reached the Casino, Derek was given the VIP treatment,"Yes sir Mr.Watsen your table is ready, they entered the Casino and walked to the High Roller section the Croupier bowed asking,"Do you prefer to play alone tonight sir?" Derek,"No we will sit at a table with the other regular players, he whispered in Sam's ear,"Hell baby I have to show you off." When they were seated he called the waiter over,"Could you fetch me a bottle of Dom Perignon champagne and two glasses." Waiter,"Yes sir immediately Mr.Watsen."The waiter placed two glasses on a table and poured,"Will that be all sir?" Derek,"No on second thought bring us four ounces of Imperial Gold Caviar, Russian style with buckwheat pancakes with a dot of sour cream and rolled, if you get it correctly there's a one hundred dollar tip in it for you."The waiter scurried off hollering,"Caviar,Caviar for Mr.Derek Watsen."

Derek,"Croupier fifty thousand in chips please lets play the game,"A thousand on 16 red." The wheel is spun the little ball falls on 17 black. Derek,"Thousand on 19 red, the wheel is spun it lands on 17 black, Derek got you that time you bastard." Waiter,"Excuse me sir your Imperial Gold Caviar"he places the order on the table saying,"I took the liberty Mr.Watsen of preparing a few of the pancakes with caviar and sour cream." Derek,"Very good my man here's an extra fifty."

Sam is taking this all in thinking,"I can see myself getting close to this mark, especially if Manny talks him into money laundering, hell I'd screw a dog if somebody paid me enough and this guy is definitely flush."

Derek picked up the dish,"Here you go sweetheart try one they are delicious. Sam picks a pancake from the dish and takes a bite, all the while she is being watched by everyone at the table."OH God, this is absolutely fabulous"Sam gushed,"Absolutely fabulous can I have another?" "All you want Sam, as long as tonight is as moving as last night."they both laughed,Sam replied,"Even better, much better."A casino Host approaches Derek,"I have made arrangements for you and your lady to dine at our Four Star Restaurant as a comp from the Casino when ever you feel free, it includes all drinks and food, please have the Croupier call Phyllis when it pleases you and I will show you to your table." Derek slides a few thousand dollars in chips too Sam,"Hell! babe try your luck."

They played for another hour, Derek won a few thousand, lost a few thousand, Sam picked up an extra five thousand slipping the chips into her pocketbook.Derek looked at Sam,"Lets get something to eat I want a large steak Pittsburg style, burned on the outside and raw inside, come on pack it in, Croupier can you buzz Phyllis and tell her we are famished." Croupier,"Yes sir Mr.Watsen." Derek flips him a five hundred dollar chip,"You have a good night." Croupier,"Thank you sir!" Derek and Sam had a five star meal,"I say we stay at the Casino tonight,I'll rent a suite and we can party hearty, maybe invite a few friends and do it up right, what say you Sam?" Sam,"Sound like a good time I know a dealer in the Casino where I can get some blow." Derek spots two couples gambling walks over to the Black Jack table,"Hey you guys up for a good time? we're looking for some company the tabs on me" the tall good looking guy answers,"Hell yea! we're up for anything, except sadism,I have some blow and reefers, where at?" Derek scans the other couple everyone looks like they are definitely ready. "Right here I rented the penthouse for the weekend, full bar we won't be disturbed guaranteed."

They all headed to the penthouse elevator, on the walk over Derek texted his Host Phyllis,"I am renting the Penthouse for the weekend, please make sure the bar is complete with my favorite liquor, send up a case of Dom Perignon and a variety of hors d'oeuvre for six, thanks."

The three couples crowded into the stainless steel elevator and immediately started stripping, by the time they reached their destination the essence of sexual pleasure permeated the walls with the musty smell of orgasms.

Sam watched in fascination as she participated in a menage a'trois with the tall good looking, built like a brick house husband and his good looking wife, the other four were in some kind of tangle doing anything and everything sexually imaginable. The elevator doors opened every one tumbled out still wreathing, panting and climaxing.Sam thought she had seen everything in the trade, but she was amazed at the sexual energy and stamina of the other couples as they went on and on having sex in every position known to man or woman,Sam looks at Derek and asks,"Jesus, Derek how in the hell do they keep on going? they are like the damned energizer bunny, he laughs answering,"Coke, maybe ecstasy, some weed all thrown in makes for a long, long screw." Just then the elevator doors open a waiter exits pushing a cart loaded with food.

Everyone is laying around naked, ignoring the waiter, who's eyes are popping out of his head and looks as if he is going to go in his pants. "Waiter put the food on the counter, you have seen nothing understand?" He shakes his head yes, as Derek hands him two hundred dollar bills. "If I hear you blabbed I will take my money back, and they will find you in a dumpster, understand?" Waiter,"Yes sir absolutely, mum is the word." The orgy went on till the sun started to rise in the east, the exhausted partakers were spread around the penthouse nude and comatose in awkward positions where they had fallen sleeping in their drug induced state. Derek rolls out of bed at ten,"Sam get up I have to tend to our guests, I want to make sure they are all still breathing." Sam,"Damn why didn't you let me sleep screw our guests, what the hell is that at the bottom of the bed?" She pulls back the sheet and there lays the waiter who delivered the food with one of the wives of the tall partier, they were still entwined in the embrace of sexual pleasure.Sam started to laugh,"I wonder what we will find when we check the other guests, what in the hell were we into last night.? I don't remember a thing."

Derek answers,"You name it and we indulged, to tell the truth my memory is blurry to say the least. I'm going out and check on the guests I just hope no one overdosed, I hate it when I have to call an ambulance." He opened the bedroom door wandering out into the main part of the penthouse there lay the prostrate forms of a Dorthy Lannone portrait, he started to count the naked bodies,"There are six out here and two more in my bed,"We started with six and somehow there are four more, I think they are part of the wait staff." he picked up the phone and rang Phyllis, "Can you order breakfast for ten and bring up some clean clothes,I'm afraid most of the my visitor's clothes need cleaning." There was the hum of the elevator as it stopped and the sound of doors sliding open, out stepped Phyllis and behind her walked two maids carrying various clothes for the naked guests."The food will be up in the next lift."She looked around at the nudes and smiled,"My, my you do party Mr.Watsen, I hope everyone is in good health." "Yea, I made sure everyone is breathing,Ok listen up everybody it is time to rise and shine food is on the way the party is over." Everyone disentangled from everyone else, groaning, bitching and headed for the bathrooms.

Phyllis just smiled saying,"The next time you have a party give me a call I could introduce you to some real cuties."

By early afternoon the guests had exited the maids were cleaning up,Sam looked at Derek,"I have some people you may be interested in meeting, it could mean putting a lot of profit on your bottom line, what do you say?"

"What the hell I love money, when and where?" Sam,"Give me a couple of hours I have to make a call and set up the meeting." Sam went into the bedroom calling her manager, "Tony, I think I have solved your problem I spent the night with this Derek Watsen, he is loaded and has connections all over the world, I think you should meet him, don't want to go into detail over the phone." Tony,"Have him meet me at my place at six tonight, I have a bundle I'm trying to make legal, see you then." Sam put the phone in the cradle,

Chapter Eighteen

am his Consort,"Derek we have a meet at six tonight is that ok with you?" Derek,"Sounds good, where is the meet?" Sam,"At an Italian Restaurant downtown, the food is delicious, at five thirty."

Derek calls down for his Porsche,"Yes sir, will be at the front door."Sam and Derek step, out of the elevator dressed to the nines,"Should be a good night, if what you tell me is true a few points per million would make me a happy man." They drove to the middle of town at a cross street, Sam said,"Pull half way down this back alley and park." Derek,"What is this, don't tell me this is the restaurant?"

Sam answers,"Don't get your balls twisted, trust me, OK!,I haven't steered you wrong yet."A large limo blinks the lights twice slowly passing Derek,Sam,"Follow them, he turns the Porsche around and follows,"What was that all about?" "Probably checked out your license plate and you, if he doesn't like what he sees you could be dead or worse." Derek,"Why don't that make me feel warm and cuddly." He follows the limo for half an hour it pulls into a Cadillac dealership and parks, he pulls in behind them his engine still running, two gorillas get out of the limo and walk to the Porsche. Body Guard,"You get out of the car the boss wants to see you, follow us." They exited and followed the bodyguards into the garage, through a backdoor and into an office. There sitting at a large table were six older men dressed as if they were in a country club at the end of the table a number of boxes overflowing with money.The gentleman sitting at the head of the table,"Sit down Derek", he looked at one of the made men,"She doesn't need to be here take her outside and make sure she keeps her mouth shut."Sam turned and walked outside leaning her hard but shapely form against the building, lit a cigarette. The Main Boss pushed the boxes full of money toward Derek,"I understand you are in the banking business there is one million dollars in the boxes we need to clean it up, I will pay you five points per million I want to see what you do with this, there is another three hundred million we need turned into bearer bonds, you try to scam me and you will die a slow and painful death, do you understand?"Derek reached for the boxes dumping them on the table,"Not that I don't trust you do you mind if I count it, where is your money machine?" The big Boss tells one of his men" Two Fingers take the gentlemen into the office so he can count the money. Two Fingers motions to Derek to follow him into the next room.

Fingers,"Machine there you know how to use?"

Derek,"Yes, can you sit over there while I count the money?"He starts to place hundred dollar bills in the machine, listening with pleasure to the whir of the Money Machine counting, counting, counting, thinking,"God,I love the smell of money, it has a scent of perfume, I know Coco Chanel must be from one of the Casinos."

Derek turns to Two Fingers,"Would you mind carrying them back into the office?" he follows behind and sits back down at the table,"The stash is ten thousand short and I will need seven points not five, I will have to run it through a bank in the islands and my contact will take at least two points as a fee to produce the Bearer Bonds."

Big Charley started to laugh,"Ha,Ha,Ha you have a big pair we will make good partners, Manny give him the ten and another hundred thousand." Derek,"There is a hundred acres for sale in Belize I will front a buy and you can sell it for a loss of seven percent to my Shell company and the proceeds will be transferred to Curacao and invested in the local banking system at ten percent, you pay me seven and recoup ten, any questions?" Big Charley,"None! I will have a hundred million wire transferred to your bank in the morning. The land purchase will be made within a week."

Derek,"Sounds like we are on the same page, there's a three million dollar estate for sale on Curacao a nice place to retire or enjoy the sun.I can handle a hundred million a month, if you give me advanced notice maybe two hundred million."

Big Charley,"Our business is done here, except for wire transfers, there is no need that we see each other again." Derek stood up stretched Fingers escorted him to the door, in the background he heard Big Charley,"It better work out or they will end up in the concrete, him and that bitch Sam." Derek climbed in the car smiled at Sam,"I guess we have a deal your friends are not people to mess with, Big Charley threatened to off both of us if we screwed up, the man has no sense of humor." Sam looked at him answering,"Screw him and the horse he rode in on, that fat bastard can't even get his dick up even when you hum on it." They drove off laughing, I Derek,"Say we rent a room and screw our eyeballs out, what do you say?"

Sam,"Sounds like a plan to me." They drove to a second rate motel and parked,"I'll get us a room and we can spend the night with the peasants." Derek just stood there with a smirk on his face,"What are you smiling about?" Sam asked,"I will take their hundred million and make another fifteen or twenty percent on the transactions before they recoup their money and you my dear are never to repeat what I just said, you understand or we will end up dead, very dead!"

Derek grabbed two bottles of champagne started for the motel room, stopping at the door,"Come on babe time to strip, snort a few lines and screw our brains out."He shed his clothes his skinny ass wiggled as he poured the coke on the table, he was skinny but his man was fourteen inches all meat, Sam got all wet just thinking about it, Thinking he has no physique but sure as hell is hung and knows how to use it." They screwed till the sun was shining its luminescence across the enraptured couple. Derek rolled off of the doggie position to shield his eyes from the rising sun,"I think It's time for a little shut eye, wake me about five" he rolls over and falls into a cocaine and sexual coma. Sam curls up next to him and sleeps the sleep of a person that has had her every sexually desire fulfilled, It's five in the PM when the couple wakes."

Sam,"Where in the hell are we?" He answers,"In some sleaze ball motel having sex, where else? time to wake and shine I'm so hungry I could eat the asshole out of a bear."

They dressed, headed for the diner down the road had steak and eggs, then Derek drove to his condo.As they entered the door man handed Derek an envelope,"Someone in a black limo left this for you Mr.Watsen"."Thanks Phil, I'll make sure you are taken care of."

When they stepped out of the lift he stopped to open the envelope, standing there reading it was from the banker on Curacao received money wire how shall I invest? it was two points short." Derek,"Would like to buy acreage in Belize, keep property for six months and sell." He folds the telegram and stuffs it his pocket, unlocks the condo door.

Derek,"Why don't you check out the clothes in the bedroom put on a negligee something sexy,I'll make us a drink."

When she walked into the living room Derek, whistled, wow babe you are a knock out I made us a couple of martinis and order up a cheese tray", they sat and drank Derek,"I have to spend time on the computer checking on my stocks, investments and the Mob's money, it will take me a couple of hours." Sam wandered around the condo, the place must be at least four thousand square feet, art on the walls,"Thinking this guy is the real thing he must be worth millions."

Chapter Nineteen

Derek walked into the living room,"What you say we have a bite to eat, I know an out of the way French Restaurant their food is to die for, why don't you freshen up we leave in an hour." Sam,"Sounds good to me I'm famished I'll be ready when you are."Sam walked into the bathroom took her phone out her pocket mated it with Derick's, she downloaded his info into her phone when she was finished called to Derek,

"Hey hon, I think you left your phone in here I'll put it on the bar so you don't forget it." He reached into his pocket no phone thinking,"I don't remember using my phone in the bathroom, OH, well no problem."

He called down,"Have my car ready in thirty minutes, I'll pick it up out front and make sure the gas tank is topped off, good thank you", he hung up.

On the drive to the Restaurant Sam looked at Derek and asked,"Did you ever think of settling down and having a family?" he looked at her and just smiled,"No not really, I have two sisters and a brother they all have kids, definitely not, I love my life never plan on marrying or having kids." They drove in silence till they arrived at the French Restaurant, when they were seated Sam,"I have to go to the powder room to freshen up, be back in a few." Sam entered the bathroom locking the door and dialed her phone, it rang a couple of times and someone picked up, "I have all of his info keep this line open so I can transfer the data any questions call me on my encrypted phone, I will get back to you as soon as I can, Diana 7." Derek,"What took you so long?, I thought you got lost."

Sam ignored his jest,"So what did you order for us, more caviar and champagne?" Derek,"Don't be a smart ass I ordered a plate of fresh seafood and Filet mignon for our main course, I'll let you order dessert."

The meal was three star, the couple ate the first course in silence when the plates were cleaned she commented on the food,"as usual you have out done your self, very good." Sitting across from Derek and Sam were two suits, the listening device on their table was recording every word of the conversation. After the meal Sam begged off returning to the condo,"I have to visit my mother, she is in a Nursing Home I'll be back on Friday." Derek,"Do you want me to drive you?" Sam,"Thanks anyway I have transportation, like I said see you in a couple of days." Sam stood waiting for her cab when it pulled to the curb the Valet opened the door and she entered, sitting in the back seat pulled a black briefcase to her and dialing the code opened it smiling,"I'll be a son of a bitch I never would have thought the Senator was involved, this case is getting stranger and stranger."

Derek left the Restaurant and drove to his condo thinking,"I wonder what Sam is up to, I'll have to check out her past there is something about her that doesn't quite make sense." He ordered his car phone,"Dial Mike Persons number" the phone rang, ring, ring,"Hello,Derek what can I do for you?"

"I need you to do a background check on a Sam O'Connell it's a woman, about thirty, five foot eight, slight built has a Boston accent, runs with the Mob we have been having an affair, there's something that doesn't click about this entire deal,I'm sending her picture to you as we speak." Parsons,"Ok, Derek I'll see what I can find on her, be back to you as soon as I can." Mike hung up, Derek,"I have a strange feeling I'm being sucked in, only can't quite figure out exactly what the end game is." Sam to the cab driver,"Stop here and leave me off." Taxi Driver,"Are you sure lady this is a rough neighborhood?"

"No sweat,I'm meeting someone." She waited leaning against the worn brick wall after fifteen minutes a black SUV drove up, stopped and the passenger door opened,"Lets go Sam we have work to do." Agent,"Did you retrieve the briefcase?" "Yes everything seems to be in order, I think the Senator should be under surveillance twenty four seven."

Pete her handler,"Relax, his house and private apartment are bugged, we have homing devices on his vehicles, he can't take a shit that we don't know when he flushes."

She started to laugh, are you serious?" Handler,"Hell when he turns on the TV we watch him, phone, etc, etc!"

"OK,OK, I'll back off." Pete pulled into a parking garage shut the car off. "This is the safe house we bought the entire building, the five floors are rented to local business, we control the three upper floors, the roof is guarded twenty four hours, we better hurry the Section Chief doesn't like to be kept waiting." Sam knocks on the Section Chief's door,"Come in Sam I have been waiting for you." She walks in and places her briefcase on the desk, Sam,"How far do you want to take this, there are a couple of Senators involved, the mob has recruited Derek Watsen to launder a few hundred million dollars he has a contact in Curacao that will clean up the money by buying land, houses and bearer bonds, from what I can glean there is an arms shipment next month being delivered to the rebels in the far East. This is bigger than we thought." Phil the Section Chief tells Sam,"You are off this case, it is getting to dangerous, your story is that you have to go to the midwest to take care of your dying mother." Sam,"What!are you kidding me? that is bullshit it took me two years undercover to get this far,I have to tell myself every time I screw this guy I'm enjoying myself so I don't puke, he is such a pompous asshole."

Section Chief,"Sam this comes from the top you have twenty four hours to cut the cord here are your orders, I'll meet you at the jet, any questions?" Sam,"No, I will be there at twenty four hundred as ordered." Section Chief,"Good as long as you understand I have nothing to do with this, we have other people in place it is going to get messy they are kicking you upstairs, so be happy."

As soon as she was outside Sam texted Derek's phone,"I have a family emergency will be out of town for a few weeks." Derek saw a text from Sam and reading the message commented,"Oh well, have to find another squeeze for tonight." Derek started the Jag heading for the Casino.He walked to the high roller section asking,"Is Phyllis here tonight?"

Croupier,"Yes Mr. Watsen."

Derek dialed her number," Phyllis see if there is the Penthouse available send me a couple of girls, you know what I like." Phyllis called back,"The Penthouse has been rented by the Jeffersons for the entire week, they are planing an orgy and drug party maybe you would be interested, some very strange but rich guests, I can set you up on the next floor down if you don't mind,I could send a couple of the girls up if you wish."

Derek,"NO,NO! I'll introduce my self to the Jeffersons, never could pass up an Orgy, what is the password?" "The Greek Way" Phyllis answered,"I will meet you at the elevator and give you the Penthouse code."

She was standing at the elevator waiting for Derek,"The code is 7878 it will take you to the Penthouse allowing entry, the price of the party is ten thousand dollars per head." The elevator doors opened and there stood four bodyguards,"Step out of the elevator please put your hands on top of your head." Derek did as he was told, one of the body guards frisked him for weapons then ran a wand to make sure that there was no hidden listening or recording devices."Please pay at the door the charge is fifty thousand dollars for the week or ten thousand per day, includes women or men, drugs, alcohol, and food."

Derek paid for the week, was handed a Toga,"Please remove your street clothes and wear the Toga."

He changed into the Toga entered the main living area the party was just getting underway, he counted at least forty guests who were all cavorting in sexual positions that would have put the Kama Sutra to shame."Wow, these are my kind of people, the Jeffersons are real swingers."

CIA Safe House;Agent,"Sam what did you find out about this Derek character?"

Sam,"This Derek has money located on every Island you can name. Has passports in twelve countries. We need to bring him in now before the Mafia plants him in the river with concrete shoes."

Agent,"Do you know where he is hiding?" Jacops,"He's in Vegas at a Sex orgy, my Agents are waiting for me to give the order to arrest the Bastard." Agent,"Do it now."

CHAPTER TWENTY

Marjorie was on the phone with Dominic,"What the hell is going on I haven't heard from you for a couple of days, has my daughter been positively connected to the murders, what about DNA testing, was she drugged?, well Dominic tell me what have you found out?"

Dominic her daughters Lawyer,"Jesus Marjorie, shut up and let me talk, your daughter Sara's blood shows she was drugged from what the Forensic Team can tell she was completely out of it for at least twelve hours, which theoretically means she was incapable of committing the murders within the timeframe the Coroner estimates the Jeffersons were murdered."

Marjorie,"So what does all that mean are they dropping charges or not?" Dominic,"It means they are letting her out on one hundred thousand dollars bail, she will have to wear an ankle bracelet." Marjorie,"That is total bullshit, what about DNA, my daughter was set up to get me out of Thailand Carl knew I was about to grab him by the balls and twist, plus he hates my ever loving guts." Dominic answers laughing,"I sure as hell never want you on my ass, you'r worse than a crazy woman when you get your teeth into someone." Marjorie raises her voice,"I want my daughter cleared, is there any DNA evidence or not, did you check into a reason why the Jeffersons were killed, did they screw over the drug supplier?, never mind I will find out on my own" click she disconnected the phone call.

Dominic looked at the phone,"She is a hellcat, I better check on the DNA results before Marjorie comes looking for me too" putting the cell phone in his pocket smiling,"Thinking what a woman."

Marjorie calls her local CIA contact,"Hello Phil, I need help the locals are still trying to tie my daughter Sara to the Jeffersons murders,I know damn well you have information or at least think you know who killed them and why." Phil,"Look Marjorie we're not supposed to get involved in domestic crimes." Marjorie screamed,"I didn't say get involved, who wanted the Jeffersons dead and why?"

Phil,"Let me look into it and I will get back to you,OK so keep your shirt on."

Next she called Natalie Simpson the District Attorney assigned to the case Marjorie,"Hello, who is this?" "This is Miss Simpson whom am I speaking to."

"You are speaking to Marjorie Swift, Sara's mother I would like to meet with you to understand why my daughter is not being released instead of having a one hundred thousand dollar bond and a GPS Bracelet following her around when she has to take a piss." Natalie looked at the phone thinking,"Who in the hell does this Marjorie Swift think she is,I'll do what ever I need to do to get a conviction." Marjorie took a deep breath saying to herself,"Calm down Marjorie, calm down,Look Natalie I just want to understand why my daughter is still under suspicion." Natalie,"I can't discuss the case with you

,but I will see you in court." Natalie hung up the phone. Marjorie was seeing red,"In court,I'll fix that bitch." When Marjorie arrived at CIA headquarters she flashed her ID and the guard let her in,"Phil is expecting you, Joe show her to his office." Joe escorted Marjorie to Phil's office and knocked on the door,"Boss Marjorie Swift is here." Phil,"Let her in." Marjorie looked around Phil's office as she sat in the chair facing his desk.

"Marjorie Swift we finally meet I have heard great things about you, what can I do for you?"

Without speaking she leaned over placing both her elbows on his desk,"Phil, may I call you Phil"."Why yes",he answers. "You know as well as I do Phil this is a Federal Matter not a domestic crime, and my daughter has absolutely nothing to do with the Jeffersons murders, they were into drug trafficking and from what I can glean arms sales to foreign buyers, so I would like a Federal warrant to be able to exclude the local authorities, period end of sentence." Phil,"Alright, alright I will do as you wish, I can't have you digging up anymore evidence, I have had phone calls from the Judge and DA. Tomorrow morning I will go see the Judge and settle the matter, now are you happy Marjorie?"

Marjorie,"Thank you,Phil as long as this cloud is lifted off of my daughters head, finally the case is going in the right direction." Phil,"I will meet you at the court house in the morning at nine and have a Federal Writ to remove the case from the local authorities."

At nine Marjorie and Phil entered the courthouse,"I called the Judge and appraised her of the Federal Writ. This case will be tried under the Homeland Terrorist Act."

The Bailiff stopped them,"May I see your Identification?" He then showed the pair into the Judges chambers."

When they entered Phil asks,"Your honor may we sit?" Judge,"Yes of course." Phil,"This case falls under the Homeland Terrorist Act that's all I can say, everything about this case is considered Top Secret, I will need all of the files from you and the District Attorney's office by this afternoon, Phil handed the Federal Writ to the Judge and a second for the DA.As soon as they left the Judge called in the Bailiff,"Release Sara Swift I am dropping all charges and inform Natalie Simpson of my finding." When Natalie heard about the Federal Writ she went spastic,"I know that Marjorie had something to do with this."

Marjorie waited outside of the local lockup waiting for her daughter Sara, the mother and daughter hugged and Marjorie kissed the tears from Sara's cheeks,"I'm taking you with me to Thailand you aren't safe here, they killed Susan after they couldn't use her anymore, anyone goes near you I will gut them and bury their bodies in the local dump." Sara,"Mom do you have to be so descriptive." Marjorie,"Hell baby you are my life I can't let anything happen to you."

The mother and daughter were picked up by a black SUV, the driver turned and greeted Marjorie,"Must feel good to have Sara back? your plane leaves in two hours for Thailand." Sam said,"God, Sam how in the hell are you?"

Marjorie reached out and hugged her,"Long time no see how have you been?" Sam,"Not bad they kicked me upstairs said I had spent too much time in the field, want me to school trainees, impart some of my knowledge"."Good luck with that, I would go bonkers in an office." The jet was waiting on the runway when they arrived."Come on sweetheart this is a twenty hour flight at least this plane has real seats that we can sleep in, not that bucket of bolts I rode coming back to the States." The flight back to Thailand was problem free, when they landed and entered the Embassy, they were greeted by the American Ambassador,"Welcome back, you must be Sara, Marjorie's daughter I have a nice apartment for you to settle in to no worry about someone trying to do you harm." Sara,"I thank you very much Ambassador for your generosity." Marjorie's phone vibrated,"I have a phone call if you would excuse me Ambassador, hello George what's the problem?"

"We spotted Carl and Henry in Laos ,but the Government Officials won't give us permission to cross the border to apprehend them, we have a drone up and following their route, it appears they will cross into Cambodia sometime tomorrow.I need a team in place to interdict when they cross into Cambodia." Marjorie,"What about the Cambodian government? For a few American dollars they will look the other way." George,"The pair has a large stash of drugs they purloined in Vietnam the word is they already have a buyer." Marjorie,"Give me an hour or two while I get my daughter settled in and I will be ready to join the team." Charley,"Sounds good they will be waiting at the hanger." The Ambassador,"Problem!" Marjorie,"No sir, just a normal everyday mission."

Chapter Twenty One

When she walked out of the Thailand Embassy there was the usual Black SUV waiting for her with the engine running, she climbed into the passenger seat,"Johnny how in the hell are you?" Johnny,"Good, real good I think we finally have the hook on those two, It's going to give me great pleasure to put the cuffs on them."

When they arrived at the strip the rest of the team was already suited and armed,"Marjorie welcome back, you were sorely missed there was no one kicking ass" Lieutenant Morrison quipped smiling.The pilot motioned to Morrison, "Lets load up, the drop has to be before dark."Hours later the sound of wheels being lowered woke Marjorie,"Must be coming in for the landing." Morrison,"Alright make sure your vests are in place, weapons locked and loaded, we will be on the ground in ten, the border is two clicks ahead, need to be set up in case they have picked up a few bodyguards on the way."

When they deplaned Marjorie climbed behind the wheel of the HUMVEE, Johnny manned the gun turret, Morrison sat next to Marjorie, the rest of the team climbed into the back, the ramp on the cargo plane was lowered, she gunned the engine there was a bump as the HUMVEE hit the ground and drove off across the landing field it's GPS locked onto the Drone sending intelligence, honed in on Carl and Henry.

Back in Laos the truck was approaching the drop off point, "How much longer Carl?, keep your shirt on Henry we should be there in half an hour." Carls satellite phone started to ring,"Hello, who in the hell is this?"

"This is General Chow, you are being observed by a CIA drone they are waiting for you to cross into Cambodia to arrest you and your Comrade Henry, I have set up a cover where your body heat cannot be detected by the drone, leave ten percent of the drugs with my Lieutenant and change vehicles, my men will continue to drive towards the border, you are to take the other truck and head due south till you come to the next dirt road take it into Cambodia, do as you are told or you will be monkey meat" CLICK he hung up the phone.Carl looks at Henry,"That… SCREW… wants ten percent of our stash, or else." Henry,"or else what?"

Carl,"Or we will be monkey meat, we have to meet his Lieutenant switch trucks, that means we are supposed to hand over one hundred thousand dollars of juice or we are dirt, screw him." Carl screams"

Henry,"Cool it Carl we are between a rock and a hard place, he could off us and take the entire stash, we don't need the Laotian Army up our asses, plus the CIA waiting in Cambodia, we just suck it up by kissing butt."

One click ahead there was a military roadblock, two solders armed with machine guns, they waved the truck over under a Lean-to, the solders showed their guns motioning Carl and Henry to exit the truck. Henry,"This is bullshit, they look like they want to do a job on us." Carl,"We have no choice." They stood under the Lean-to with their hands in the air, the Lieutenant called to Carl,"Carl put your hands down I'm not going to kill you the General said you were to leave twenty percent of the drugs." Carl went white,Henry grabbed him by the shoulder whispering in his ear,"Shut up, give him what he wants and let's get the hell out of here, before he changes his mind."

Carl reluctantly removes the drugs from the van, the Lieutenant brings out a scale weighing them, the twenty percent is removed and placed in the jeep the Lieutenant,"My men will drive your van no farther than the border, you must leave now or there will be consequences, I will not be able to control my men you understand?" Without speaking Carl and Henry load the remaining stash in their truck.Henry drove leaving a trail of dust behind them, drove till they reach the dirt road turning right.Henry is the first to speak,"Jesus, I thought we had it for sure, the Lieutenant made sure he took care of himself." Carl was still fuming,"God damned, Gooks everybody wants a piece of the pie!"

Then he starts laughing,"My asshole was so tight I could have driven a railroad spike." Carl,"I need a large drink and the nearest whore house."

The CIA in Cambodia were all set to capture Carl and Henry, Marjorie was salivating at the thought,"That son of a bitch had tried to frame my daughter for murder, when we capture Carl I am going to personally have my revenge."

Marjorie is thinking as she sharpens her Ontario MK 3, hummed to herself,"Thinking God I hope he shits himself when I cut him." Morrison cut into her revery,"They are one click out everybody get ready." The CIA Team could see a dust cloud being stirred up as the truck approached, it looked as if it was going to cross into Cambodia, then it screeched to a halt throwing gravel and dirt. Every one stood up,"What in the hell is going on."Morrison watched as the solders dismounted from the truck lit cigarettes lounging against the van and talking,"We have been made this is a cover, those two switched trucks they are probably still in Cambodia, as I speak."

Morrison called the drone pilot,"Send the drone south along the border, they have eluded us, see if there is another road, let me know if you see anything, over and out."

"Let's go people we have to hustle if we're going to catch them."

Marjorie drove like a mad woman, swearing under her breath, "Got to catch the bastards, got to catch the bastards, can't let them get away." Morrison looks at her and asks,"What in the hell are you muttering about. Jesus, Marjorie you are driving me nuts, slow down before you wreck the HUMVEE, I'm too young to die." She slows down pulling over on the berm of the road. Marjorie,"God damned it Morrison they escaped again they have nine lives, the next time I have those two in my sights they are dead."

Morrison's satellite phone rings,Drone Pilot,"Spotted them about fifty clicks east of you they are moving pretty fast, you will never catch them, the drone is running out of fuel, I have to bring it home sorry guys." Morrison checks the HUMVEE GPS,"We know where they are right now it should take us an hour to drive to their present location, hopefully they will stop to rest."In Cambodia, Carl,"Henry look for someplace we can relax, we have been pounding the road for three days"."There's a bar pull over maybe we can trade trucks then relax for a couple of days." Henry pulled up to the front they walked into the bar,"Can we have a couple of beers and something to eat that Fish Amok looks good we'll take two, the two men devoured the Fish Amok in a few minutes,"Damned that was good, we need to get rid of the wheels now, the hair is raised on the back of my neck I know the CIA is looking for us, the bastards never give up. For all we know that drone is still tracking us." Henry walks to the bar,"We have a truck we would like to trade or do you have something we could buy? We would pay good money as long as it is kept quiet, understand?"

The bartender,"I have an Toyota Prius for twenty thousand dollars out back." Henry,"That is pretty steep I'll pay you twelve thousand, no can do fifteen, thirteen, fourteen thousand that's it." Bartender,"OK, how you pay cash, how about drugs?, I'll throw in two ounces of coke what do you say?" Bartender smiles they shake hands,"Here is keys to car now, you pay as agreed."

Henry throws the car keys to Carl,"We have a deal our friend here wants his payment out of our stash. Carl walks out the back door to the Prius, puts the key in the ignition car starts the engine is purring,"Sounds like it will take us to Phnom Penh" he drives the truck around the back of the Bar places the coke under the rear seat, drives the Prius around front, calls to Henry,"Lets go brother times a wasting.Henry bounded out the door,"The tanks full we need to shit and git before they catch up to us."

Carl,"I gave our contacts in Phnom Penh a heads up we will be there tonight with a stash and I need it on the street by morning."

CIA: Morrison,"There's a Bar sitting off the road, we should stop and ask if they have seen Carl and Henry",Marjorie pulled the HUMVEE into the stone parking lot and Morrison jumped out and entered, he walked to the bartender laying pictures of Carl and Henry on the bar,"Have you seen these two men today?" The bartender barely looked at the pictures, answered,"Me no see anytime."Morrison placed a fifty down, then another fifty. "Maybe I see them today." Morrison,"What time?" Bartender, "Around three they traded the HUMVEE for my Prius and left."

Morrison jumped into the HUMVEE,"They are three hours ahead of us, let's go." Marjorie,"Shit Morris they will be in Phnom Penh well before we can catch up to them."

Chapter Twenty Two

Carl pulled over just before they reached Phnom Penh, blowing the car horn three times, out of the jungle emerged four armed thugs,Carl rolled down the window,"There is a HUMVEE following us I want you to hold it up long enough to give us a a couple hours lead and I don't care what you do understand?" they all shook their heads yes,"Good we understand each other, you get paid tonight at the rendezvous."

Marjorie had changed places behind the wheel, Johnny was driving on a straightaway,"What the hell is that up ahead?, I thought I saw something alongside the road."

He slowed down, hollered to the crew in the back one of you man the machine gun!, there may be an ambush ahead." Just then the roar of a machine gun and the sound of lead ricocheting off the HUMVEE'S armor,"Shoot the son of a bitches now, before one of us is killed",the M134 Mini-gun answered, chopping down the palm trees sending them careening on the attackers, causing the attackers to retreat in panic,"Bastards are like worms they are everywhere, Marjorie jumps out of the HUMVEE firing over the hood,"I'm tired of this shit, I say we kill the bastards and take scalps, she "SCREAMS I... want Carl."

One of the attackers drops his weapon putting up his hands Marjorie, still in her kill mode cuts the poor bastard in half, reloads to snuff out the others. Morrison jumps out of the HUMVEE grabbing the weapon out of her hands, "Enough, stop now!, Her eyes were glazed over,"Get hold of yourself" he slapped her,"Do that again and I will have your ass back in the states so fast your head will spin." Marjorie wiped the sweat running down her face,"Sorry Morrison I just flipped out, won't let it happen again.Those two just have me so FRIGGING frustrated I could scream." Morrison,"Keep that shit up and you will get one of us killed." Morrison,"You know better, now let's get going, the drone is still tracking the Prius. The base thinks they have stopped for the night or have switched cars, either way we have them on the run." Henry pulled the Prius into a shielded concrete bunker,"That drone won't be able to find us in the bunker,I say we unload the coke then, let one of the crew drive the Prius into Phnom Penh and ditch it." Carl and Henry cut the drugs with talcum powder and for good measure throw in a pinch of fentanyl, Henry laughs,"That ought to give our customers a real buzz for the money." Carl,"Tell Akra to bring in the girls to start bagging the stash, we have twenty kilos of pure coke add the same weight of talcum powder a little fentanyl and there is forty thousand, twenty dollar bags." Henry,"If it hadn't been for that greedy Lieutenant, and General, we would have a couple million dollars of product to put on the street." Carl calls Akra,"I need a dozen boys, give them fifty bags each. Their take is four dollars per bag and one dollar for your trouble, if you want a bigger cut take another fifty bags and go sell them."

Akra bows to Carl,"Thanks boss, I need the money."

Carl, "Don't stand there get your ass moving so I can make money."

It was midnight the hum of the generator droned on and on, keeping the lights burning as the women filled bag after bag of the product then placing them in containers of one hundred bags each. The Coke factory hummed with activity till dawn.

The generator gave a groan, belched smoke sputtering to a stop, the lights slowly dimmed then shut down, it was pitch black. Henry,"That's all for tonight." The women removed their masks and changed clothes, leaving the nights dust laying on the floor.Carl looked at Akra asking,"Are the couriers here?" Akra answers,"Yes boss." Carl,"Good have them sign for the Bags. I want this stuff made available from here to Thailand in every tourist and expat hangout there is, you understand?" Carl walked into the office attached to the Coke factory, Henry was sitting at the computer keeping track of the distribution of the product, he looked up as Carl stopped standing over him,"Well, we have ten thousand bags in circulation by the end of the week if things go good the entire batch will be gone"Henry mused. Carl,"Good, we need to screw out of here, I have a feeling our boy from Vietnam is looking for us, the informant in Laos said he is coming our way with at least six guns."

Chapter Sixteen

General there is a Mr. Vong to see you,"Tell him I will see him in twenty minutes and please send in Captain Kapono I need to speak with him. Captain Kapono enters the Generals office stands at attention, salutes,"Captain you remember the product we confiscated awhile back?" "Yes,General it has been taken care of." General,"I want anyone who was involved to be removed from the site immediately, you will be informed when to return." Captain Kapono,"Very good General."

Mr. Vong sitting in his Range Rover watched as Captain Kapono ordered his men to climb into a Duce and a half then drive away.He wonders,"What the hell is the General up to." A guard exits the General's office,"The General will see you now." Mr.Vong signals to his men to dismount and follow. The guard locks and loads his weapon,"Please,Mr.

Vong only you will be allowed to speak with the General." Before answering Vong glanced around noticed a number of troops had encircled the vehicles and spotted two machine gun posts. Vong," Very good Sergeant my men will stay in the vehicles, please show me the way." The building could use paint it was a typical military post, all military green.

Mr.Vong thought,"I wonder if the General knows our friends?" The Sergeant knocked on the door,"It's open please enter Mr. Vong." The Sergeant opens the door allowing Vong to enter he bows to the General who is sitting behind his desk smoking a large cigar, the General looks up, "Please, sit Mr. Vong, what can I do for you?"

"I am looking for two Americans they are friends of mine." "Really and do you have business with them?" Vong,"You could say that, it is personal." General notes,"That is interesting a while back I was informed that two Americans passed through our great Mother land, but I have no other information as to Henry's and Carl's whereabouts."

"That is a shame, the reward would be great if someone could tell me where they are." The General sat upright,"And what is the size of this reward." Vong,"Say ten thousand American dollars." The General replied,"That is a shame twenty thousand would help my memory."

Vong,"Exactly what I had in mind twenty thousand." The General butted his cigar, stood up,"We have a deal, they are in Cambodia the word is from here all the way to Thailand is being flooded with Cocaine. They are holed up in a concrete bunker a few clicks over the border." Mr. Vong reached into his coat pocket and removed two packets of one hundred dollar bills placing them on the Generals desk.The General pulled open his desk drawer removing a map.

"This will allow you to find your friends,I had my men keep track of them just in case a friend like yourself could afford to pay for their location." The General just smiled and sat back in his chair. Mr. Vong climbed back into his brand new Range Rover, he handed his driver the map,"When I find those two bastards, I will screw them up so bad their own mothers won't be able to recognize them."

Two days prior at the bunker,Carl,"Henry I just sold the rest of the stash, we need to get the hell out of here I have that strange feeling on the back of my neck our friends from "NAM" are coming for a visit very soon."

Chapter Twenty Three

CIA:Marjorie walks into the Section Chiefs office,"I think we may have a problem, our satellite has been keeping surveillance on Vong from Vietnam, last we knew he was traveling through Laos. So we sent up a drone to track him,It appears he is traveling with about a dozen men heading toward Cambodia." Jimmy one of the CIA agents walked into the office,"What the hell is going on the area is awash in coke laced with fentanyl, people are overdosing on the green in Bangkok, the Thai police have asked for our help." Marjorie,"There is a rumor that our friends Carl and Henry killed a few of Vong's men when they knocked over his stash of drugs and now he's looking for revenge."

DRUG DEALER: Vong,"We are almost to the bunker, pull over,I want three men on foot to circle the rear of the bunker to keep them from trying to escape through the back, the rest of the men stay with the van."The Range Rover took a backroad it was positioned to attack the west side of the bunker. There was the sound of the van approaching from the east, they were going to make a run at the front of the bunker with machine guns and grenades.As the van pulled breast of the front of the bunker there was a loud flash and the van was thrown into the air.It landed on it's side rolling over and over, the sound of men screaming in pain, as the broken van slid to a stop against the side of the bunker crushing the top with a earsplitting sound of death. The surviving occupants were attempting to escape the carnage when the van exploded in a huge fireball drowning out the agonizing screams of the survivors who died instantly. Vong,"The no good son of a bitches, I will kill those two slowly, I'll roast them over an open flame and watch as the flesh peels off their bones. I will let them suffer, begging for death." His driver asks, "What now boss?" Vong,"We regroup, hire a few locals to track them down wait for our chance, I should have known better than underestimate those two."

Back at the American Embassy in Bangkok Marjorie was monitoring the camera on the drone,"I'll be a "Frigging Bitch" there is a fire fight occurring in Cambodia right under our noses. That must be where they are hiding our boy Vong was trying to take revenge for his murdered men." She did a double take as there was a bright flash and the attacking van flew into the air and came crashing down into the bunker. "Jesus Christ, they hit a land mine,O'Shit! We have a full blown gang war on our hands."She downloaded the film projected it on the wall screen,"I know the crew will want to have a look at this."

Carl and Henry opened a bottle of Champagne poured themselves each a glass and toasted,"Here's to us that Vong never knew what hit him, he will probably run back to Vietnam with his tail between his legs. We should be in the clear I'll meet with our mole tonight, he can let us know what is going on at the Embassy he's expensive, but well worth it." Henry,"We can't cross into Thailand if we are caught the CIA will put us on the first plane to the states." Carl,"Henry keep your cool, our Mole is in Cambodia carrying a Diplomatic Pouch, we will have to change our location tonight I'm sure we are being watched."

Marjorie and Morrison left the strategy meeting,"We have our work cut out for us,"That Carl and Henry are like a shit storm in a tornado, everyone gets covered in do-do and they walk away smelling like roses."They both laugh,"I say we get something to eat, we have to meet the Thai Special Police this afternoon. An informant thinks he knows where those two are holed up.The CIA wants to be present when the takedown occurs. We have been given the honor of arresting them."

Later that night Carl and Henry are waiting to meet their snitch,"You sure this isn't a trap, this spy garbage isn't my cup of tea","Keep cool Henry I bought this perp he is well paid." That's him over there carrying the brief case. Henry circle to the left to make sure the coast is clear, I'll stay here and keep watch." Carl signals with his flashlight, the figure stands up and walks toward them.

Perp,"I only have a couple of minutes to talk they think I'm still in the hotel, the CIA has a million dollar bounty on your heads. One of your people has alerted the Thai and Cambodian police as to your whereabouts, they are going to try to arrest the two of you and make the exchange at the border. My advice is get the hell out of here and back to the jungle." Carl and Henry just look at each other, the noose is tightening,Henry reacts,"If they catch us we are going away for a long, long time."

In Vietnam Vong is irate,"I want those two num-nuts found and crucified, not only did they steal my stash, killed my men but flooded the market with my coke making a few million. Then to top it off tried to kill me, I repeat find Carl and Henry, kill, maim, bring back body parts, drain their blood.I don't care just get them out of my hair."Quan his Chief Lieutenant,"I am on it boss, I hired two dozen locals they will do whatever it takes, we captured Akra their main distributor last night after a few hours of torture he agreed to let us know the next time Carl or Henry contact him"."Can you trust him or is he just blowing smoke?"."We have his wife and kid if he tries to screw with us they are dead meat" Quan answers.

Carl and Henry are still on the green when Carls cell phone rings,"Who in the Hell is that?,Henry asks,"It's Akra"."What do you need I told you not to call me unless it's an emergency." Akra,"Sorry boss, we have to meet can't talk over the phone, when and where?"

Carl,"Let me think about it and I will get back to you." Carl hangs up,"What do you think?" Henry,"I think we are being set up, there are rumblings that Vong wants us dead period. We throw away our phones, get a couple of burners, I say we disappear for a couple of months, let the heat cool down."

CIA Agent Morrison,"Marjorie we have a ping on their cell it looks like Carl and Henry are in Phnom Penh." There is a knock on Marjorie's office door...WHAT!?" The Agent monitoring the satellite walks in,"I think we have a mole in the Embassy when the satellite picked up Carls phone we also picked within a few feet of Carl, the cell of our Courier who is delivering a Diplomatic Pouch to one of our undercover Agents in Cambodia"the Agent explains." Marjorie,"Don't let him disappear under the radar, advise our undercover Agent to be aware there may be a leak and we will take care of the problem when the courier returns to Bangkok."

She turns to Morrison shaking her head,"Jesus, who can be trusted it seems everyone has a price. Loyalty is non existent." Morrison asks,"Do we have assets in Phnom Penh?" "Yes, around Phnom Penh about a dozen" Morrison,"Tell them to see if they can get a fix on Henry and Carl, maybe with any luck we can apprehend those two and smuggle them into the States before the Cambodian government gets into the act. With all the trouble the US is having with their government, they may arrest Carl and Henry and then let them escape for a price."

CHAPTER TWENTY FOUR

"I gave Akra a phony location on where we were headed." Carl asks,"Henry do you have any info on how we are going to get into Myanmar?"Henry answers,"There is a fishing boat leaving at one in the morning I bribed the captain to let us board a couple of hours ahead of time.He will take us to the Thai border. It's not far to Myanmar, we should be safe in a couple of hours, we leave from Kom Som." Carl,"Ok, let's get going before the Thai Police spot us and we are arrested." Henry,"Just follow my lead."The pair drive a couple of hours. "Where in the hell are we?,I don't see any water or fishing boats." Henry,"Trust me, turn right here." There is a blinding light,Carl,"We have been sold down the river we have to make a run for it." Henry,"Keep your pants on that is our ride."

Carl,"What in the hell are you talking about, are you throwing me under the bus?" Henry,"Just pull over it's cool I set this up, everyone will be at the port to take us down, meanwhile we will be on our way to Myanmar by plane,"I rented a Piper Aztec the pilot is familiar with the southern part of the country, he flies contraband there all the time we'll be in Myanmar before sunrise. Carl parked the car, Henry placed C4 in the front seat and set the timer. They walked to the plane and boarded. The pilot greeted them,"Howdy gentlemen, I'll have you in Myanmar before sun rise."

Morrison,"We have the port locked down." The Captain of the fishing boat said, Henry paid him twenty thousand dollars to ferry the two of them to Myanmar tonight, make sure our people stay in the shadows, don't want to spook them." Marjorie,"I sure hope we will finally get our hands on those two, I want to see Carl piss himself when I threaten to disembowel the bastard." The warm rays of the sun shining through the car window woke her with a start.Marjorie,"Are they here?, she mumbled,"Nope,I think the bastards outwitted us again, they must have been tipped off God knows where they could be by now" Morrison answered. Marjorie,"Back to the grind we need to question the courier when he comes back to the Embassy, he is playing a dangerous game." Morrison notes,"I have to find out who hired him, maybe we have more than one mole in the Embassy."Morrison blinked the car lights signaling the stakeout was over. He started the car heading back to Thailand.

CHAPTER SEVENTEEN

In Myanmar the Piper Aztec bounced a couple of times on landing. The Pilot hollered,"Lets go gentlemen flights over, time to pay up." Henry,"As soon as our man shows up he should have been here by now" the pilot turned in his seat holding a Beretta M9,"Now boys don't screw with me I want payment now, not later. Cough up the hundred thousand you promised or you two are dead and I'll collect the million dollar reward on your heads."

Henry answers,"No problem, my friend it's in my bag, I was just kidding." Henry reaches for the bag sitting at his feet slowly unzips it, meanwhile motioning to Carl to go for cover. He wraps his hand around a "Glock 18" slowly brings it up to waist height and empties the entire magazine through the seat in one burst.The pilot's body jerks like a puppet on a string, as blood spirts from his mouth, his eyes wide in surprise falls to the cabin floor with a loud thump.

He looks at Carl,"You still in one piece, imagine that asshole threatening us, he had a lot of balls.I say we burn the plane. I'll set it up to ignite an hour after we're on the road." Henry placed the C4 against the fuel tank and set the timer,"OK, Brother lets move out the truck is in the trees, we have to be out of here by sunrise."

Carl looks at Henry and quips,"You never cease to amaze me Henry, you are one cold blooded bastard.You planned to kill him from day one." He answers,"You think I was going to leave a witness, with half the country looking for us, HELL NO!"

The truck was camouflaged with a netting, Henry removed it and climbed into the drivers seat,"Lets go Carl times a wasting, I need to change into my disguise." Carl,"What do you have up your sleeve now?" Henry"You'll see, when I'm done we will disappear into the population."Henry looked in the rear view mirror and smiled as the rising sun was eclipsed by a fire ball in the distance,Thinking,"Good riddance, if that pilot thought I would pay him a hundred thousand dollars he must have had a wet dream,"The pair drove till they approached a Holistay.

Henry pulled in,"We'll stay here today then head for the Capitol tonight." When they entered the room Henry went directly into the bathroom laying out the items necessary to complete his disguise, he brewed a pot of tea, laid out an orange robe, shaved his head, rubbed his face, hands and bald head to brown his skin, looked into the mirror smiling,"I dare them to recognize me or Carl when I'm done."

He called to Carl,"Hey brother get your fat ass in here so I can get you made up.You are going to be my begging companion." Carl,"Henry you are one pain in my ass." Henry,"Stop moaning let's get this over with, we have to meet with the Chinese in seven days to complete the arms deal or our goose will be cooked. If we screw this deal up we will be toast." Henry smiled.Carl stripped off his clothes leaving on his shorts, Henry soaked a sponge in the pot of tea,Henry stepped back when he was done to admire his handy work."Carl was brown from head to toe, Henry handed Carl a pair of brown eye contact lenses,"We have to cover those blue eyes and here's your beggars bowl you walk behind me and beg for money, when we get to the Monastery the monks will smuggle us into Thailand where the Chinese meet will take place.Lets go my friend times a waisting. It's a three days walk to the Monastery."

CIA office, Manny knocked on Marjorie's office door, "Come in, any news on the two fugitives?"."Yes, there is chatter that a weapons shipment is coming out of China and our boys are meeting somewhere in Thailand to make the swap in the next couple of days." Marjorie,"That doesn't give us very much time to organize a response, send up a couple of drones maybe we will get lucky and check on any tramp steamers due to dock in the next couple of days, OK Manny, let me know when you have something." Marjorie dialed her handler,"Charley this is Marjorie we have a ping on Carl and Henry, our intel is they are meeting with the Chinese to pick up an arms shipment." Charley,"We have to be careful I don't want any direct conflict with the Chinese, my thinking is we allow them to hand over the weapons to our boys, then we arrest them and deport the two miscreants back to the states and prosecute them for murder. That way it won't be necessary to reveal any secret information as to how and why we were able to capture Carl and Henry, you get my drift?"

Marjorie,"I under stand completely Sir, I would like Morrison to be my backup if possible." Charley,"He's in the Far East right now on a secret mission I'll have to contact the Office to see if he can be spared for the operation."

Hanging up the phone she raises from her desk and walks out into the operations center and leans over Manny."How are you doing, picking up any more chatter?"

Manny looks over his glasses and smiles,"Have the name of the ship that's carrying the cargo it's the Golden Swan if you believe that shit."

Chapter Twenty Five

"When and where is she supposed to dock?" As far as I can tell it's the Port of Samui, my intel is that the cargo will be offloaded out to sea and brought in on a much smaller craft that will be turned over to rebels after the money passes hands." Marjorie,"Pass this message down the line, we are not to directly confront the Chinese under any circumstance only target the vessel carrying the weapons after the transfer,UNDERSTOOD? Send one of the drones to scout how far out the Golden Swan is." Her encrypted cell is ringing,"Hello, what is the word can I have Morrison for backup on this one?" Charley,"He will be flying in Wednesday you have twenty four hours to brief him on the mission."

"General Hong our Gaofen-1 satellite is tracking the Golden Swan it is two days out." Hong,"Very good Comrade keep me informed as long as the ship is in International waters the CIA will not act. I am sure they are aware it is carrying illegal cargo, It will keep them in suspense, they are waiting for the cargo to be offloaded before they act." Comrade,"I do not understand General."

"Neither country wants a direct confrontation so we play a chess game to see who can check mate the other.I find the game quite stimulating."

General Hong,"Call the Captain of the Golden Swan on our encrypted line and inform him to stay in International waters till further notice." Comrade,"Yes General."

In Myanmar,"Jesus Henry, how much further is this Temple? these frigging sandals are killing my feet and I feel like a stupid fool holding a bowl begging money." Henry,"Carl stop crying like a little girl, the Monastery is an hours walk let me do the talking.We don't need the Monk getting spooked." Henry was at home with the food stands, the exotic smells of the spices, the din of vendors selling their wares, exhaust of motor bikes, the smell of human sweat."God, I love the feel and aroma of human flesh, maybe when this is all over I will retire here."Henry mused.

Carl,"Lets get this shit over with my feet are killing me." Henry,"Only another ten minutes and we will be there, I'll call the head Monk to let him know we are just a couple of minutes away, so let's get a move on Carl."

There was a slight breeze that caused the air to swirl causing tiny dust devils the color of crimson enhanced by passing motor bikes and the tramping of thousands of feet resulting in the pair having to cover their faces with scarves to keep their lungs from filling with the talcum powder like dust.

Henry stood at the Monastery steps waiting for Carl to catch up, he was breathing heavily as he approached,

"God damned it Henry, what's the big hurry?" he asked as he wiped the red dust and sweat from his corpulent brow."Henry, "Easy brother you wipe too hard and you will give your disguise away.Just blot don't rub,OK." Carl,"Yea,Yea I hear you,"He looked up as the head Monk traversed the steps toward the pair,"Welcome and Peace be with you Brothers the treasure of life is within your grasp, please enter and sit with me so we may partake of a cool drink." Henry and Carl both bowed following the head Monk into the Monastery, when they were ushered into his private quarters he closed the doors,"I have a message from General Hong, the package is sitting in international waters, there is a craft waiting for you at Meyek to off load the weapons, you can stay here tonight and I will have one of my men guide you in the morning." Sunrise they washed the grit from their bodies dressing in farmers clothes, at ten a small truck parked at the rear of the Monastery,"Your guide and bodyguards are here, when you get to the boat there will be some bodies to help you unload the weapons and transport them to the rebels in Thailand. The Chinese government wants to keep that part of Thailand in turmoil, it will keep the Thai Military busy while we smuggle drugs and set up our slave trade."

Carl,"What do you sense Henry, are we being used or is this legit? you know the Chinese military has very little love for us." Henry,"I have a feel they need us to deliver the weapons, after the delivery that's another story.I say we get paid prior to the delivery, have the money sent to our Swiss account. Otherwise we refuse to complete the contract." Carl walked into the Monks private rooms the Monk was praying to his Buddha,"Pray tell what are you doing? we are know this Monastery is a Chinese front."

Monk,"I still practice my beliefs when I am out of sight of my Chinese masters, what do you want? speak and get out."

Carl stood for a moment,"We want our advance sent to a Swiss account prior to leaving today or we walk."

Monk,"I will have the pair of you shot dead, you complete the delivery or else."

"Don't threaten me you asshole I would as soon slit your throat and piss on your grave, now pay us or I will burn this stinking Temple or Monastery or what ever you call it to the ground with you and your boys still in it." Carl threatened his voice a deep growl. Henry stood at the doorway armed with an Uzi machine gun, he smiled pointing it at the Monk,"Please, please send our money to this Swiss bank I really don't want to kill you."

Carl looked at the floor and the carpet was soaked where the Monk was standing his knees were shaking, he had urinated on himself,"Please don't kill me I am only doing as I was ordered" Henry hollered,"Tell General Hong, we get paid or the deal is off, do it now or I will off you."

Monk,"They will kill me." Carl,"Look Comrade or whatever your title is I won't ask again, I will alert the CIA and blow this deal. You schmucks are screwing with the wrong boys."

The Monk dialed his cell phone and called General Hong the phone rang twice when the General answered,"Hello, what do you want?" General,"I told you not to bother me until the delivery is complete."

Chapter Twenty Six

CIA,"Our intel is the tramp steamer Golden Swan is carrying the weapons, the ship is anchored in International waters, we can't touch her until the she crosses the twelve mile base line." Marjorie sets the phone on its cradle and smiles thinking,"Now, I have those two in my net all I have to do is close it then they are mine" she could taste the sweet sense of vengeance. One of the controllers hollered, "I have the drone in place to destroy the Golden Swan is it a go." Marjorie screams,"Hell no! I need those two alive to put on trial in the States stand down, all I need at present is surveillance of the ship.Let me know when the pickup takes place.We have assets waiting for when they attempt to cross into Thailand with the weapons."

RUSSIAN Mafia,"Comrade there is chatter all over the internet, something is going down tonight" Ivan replied, "Shit we have a shipload of women being delivered."Can you pinpoint if it is CIA, FBI, Chinese, or drug traffic in this part of the world it could be anyone of them or all of them."His radio man answers,"There is something about a Golden Swan, I am attempting to figure out if it is a code word for some type of covert operation." Ivan thinks for a minute,"The name sounds familiar check the ship register if you find something get back to me ASAP. I can't afford to have this deal screwed up we have two houses ready to go and a load of coke to distribute so hurry, hurry."

Henry could hear General Hong screaming obscenities in Chinese, he started to laugh he knew he had him by the short hairs,"Money now or the deal is off I'll have the ship captain drop the whole damned load in the ocean. Tell him he has ten minutes to transfer the two million to our account starting now." The Monk was sweating bullets,"Please General my people need the weapons."

Henry was in contact with their inside man at the bank, he would know immediately when the money was deposited.

Monk,"He is sending the payment as we speak, Henry looked at Carl, giving him the thumbs up,"We have it locked up." Henry smiles.

Carl,"Where's the truck? I need six men to help us unload and transport the cargo, the only people to have weapons will be Henry and Carl the rest of the crew will be unarmed if I find any of your men carrying weapons I will personally shoot them, do you understand!" The Monk bowed to Carl,"Yes, your words are law."

A Duce and a half pulled around to the rear of the Monastery Henry climbed into the front seat and rode shotgun with the driver, Carl sat in the rear with the help, both men were armed with Uzi Machine Guns. Henry aimed the Uzi at the drivers head just smiling. Henry commanded,"Lets move brother we have to be there by midnight."The blacktop turned into a dirt road twenty miles outside of the city.Henry was getting frustrated,"This shitty road is slowing us down, stop here and fill this pig up with gas." They traveled for another one hundred clicks,"Pull over here and park." Driver,"But boss we're still ten minute drive from the boat." Henry,"I said PARk... now!" The driver parked the truck, Henry poked the driver in the ribs with his Uzi and called too Carl,"Carl,I say we walk to the boat we will have our companions walk point, I don't trust anyone I want to make sure we aren't being set up." Carl stood at the back of the truck holding his machine gun and watched as the crew exited the vehicle.He waived the machine gun,"Line up next to the truck." Henry,"Have them all walk ahead of us I'll take the right, you take the left just keep them in front of us." When the crew was within sight of the boat.Henry cautions,"Everyone stay where they are If anyone moves Carl will make you dead." He crouched low as he approached the boat, hearing voices stopped, there were four armed men guarding the boat."I wonder if they are friend or foe." He dials the cell phone,"Carl have the rest of the crew show themselves to the guards watching the boat be careful I smell a rat."Carl and Henry waited in the thicket of palms while the crew exposed themselves to the guards.

The head man placed his hand on his Glock motioning the laborers to move to the front of the vessel,"On the ground all of you. Ahab check them for weapons."Ahab stood the crew up one at a time and frisked them then made the men lay face down in the sand,"They are all clean boss." "OK, everyone get into the boat we have a freighter to unload, by the way where are the two Americans they were supposed to be with you?" Henry stepped out of the woods pointing his Uzi at the leader,"Who in the hell are you and what do you want? this is my gig so go screw off or I will waste the bunch of you" he retorted. Ahab,"You must be Henry, look I am only doing what I was paid for so keep your shorts on,General Hong wanted to make sure the delivery was made as planned." Henry,"Tell Hong he owes me another fifty thousand when this is all over for his bullshit." Ahab,"I would keep General Hong on my good side if I were you, he makes a very, very dangerous enemy." Henry ignores the remark, his phone rings he looks at the screen it reads" all is ready."

"OK, let's get on board the Golden Swan is sitting off shore waiting for us to unload the cargo." The crew climbed into the fishing trawler Henry revved the engines and they started out to sea.One of the crew hollered,"I'm picking up the Golden Swan on the radar, she's about three miles out."When they were within sight of the Golden Swan Henry gave the call sign,"X- RAY,BRAVO",ship answered back,"We copy make contact in fifteen minutes." The Trawler pulled alongside the Golden Swan,"Heave to and drop the fenders, when the cargo is set on our deck make sure every pallet is chocked we are in rough seas I don't need the cargo shifting and killing half the crew, SO MOVE IT, MOVE IT."Henry smiled thinking,"I always wanted to captain my own ship. When the trawler was loaded, they cast off and started for the shore. Carl was standing on the prow of the trawler with a pair of binoculars. Henry walked up to him asking,"What in the hell are you looking for."Carl,"I have a feeling we are being watched." Henry,"Watched how?" Carl,"I would give you five to ten the CIA has a drone surveilling every thing we are doing.I just have that creeping feeling down my spine that something isn't right."

Chapter Twenty Seven

American Embassy CIA,"We have the Golden Swan and the Trawler on the "ARGUS-IS" drone I am flying it at 20,000 feet, the weapons have been off loaded the Trawler is heading for shore, what are your orders Agent Swift? keep surveillance or take the Trawler out." I want you to let me know when they unload the cargo and start into the jungle, we will wait until the caravan crosses into Thailand and connects with the rebels, then and only then will the decision be made to kill or let them live, Susan tell Agent Johnson I need to speak to him, please close the door on your way out."

Johnson taps on the entrance window, Marjorie waves him into her office,"Sit down we need to talk, there is a spy in our group maybe more than one. Johnson opens his mouth to reply, Marjorie holds her finger to her lips signaling do not speak,"We need to go to the safe room before I elaborate." She had one of her people wand the safe room just in case," Marjorie,"Has anyone been in here to make renovations lately?" The agent answered,"No Ma'am it's been at least six months." Marjorie,"what about new furniture?"

Johnson,"New table and chairs last week." Marjorie,"Have them removed, NOW!" After the furniture was replaced Marjorie and Johnson finally sat to have their conference. Marjorie started the conversation,"I have received information from DC that they are picking up chatter that emanates from our Embassy here in Bangkok. They suspect it is someone in the audio surveillance section. I want you to take charge from the present Audio Director, isolate her, from the rest of the workers, feed each of them false information, their phones will be monitored, computers, plus any devices used to collect sensitive information." Johnson asks,"What about the present Director?"

Marjorie,"She is being transferred to the states this weekend, keep this hush-hush, her plane leaves tomorrow at five am." Johnson stands up and salutes,"Yes Ma'am, I sure don't want to get on your bad side Boss." Marjorie,"let me know when they are set up I don't need sarcasm.Do a good job or you will find your ass in the states, toot sweet." Alone Marjorie flips open her encrypted phone, it rings twice a secretary answers" Hello, what can I do for you Agent Swift?" Majorie,"Have Morrison meet me in the safe area when he arrives at the Embassy,Please!" Secretary,"He is on a mission and is supposed to return by four this evening, I will give him the message when he returns."

Marjorie looks at her watch,"It's two o'clock Morrison won't be here for at least two hours, she calls upstairs,"This is Agent Swift I'm going to lunch and I want an armed escort, will be up in twenty have him meet me at the main entrance." She places the phone in it's cradle thinking,"That's all I need Is some Russian with a screw loose trying to off me." "She had felt for quite awhile that there was a target on her back. She met Niran her escort at the entrance. Marjorie, "Niran, how are you, what are you carrying?" Niran,"I have a Glock and a leg weapon what is the matter, has there been chatter about a kidnapping or attempted assassination of a staff member?"Niran questions."No!I just don't want to take any chances, too many things going on."

Russian Drug Cartel;Ivan,"We have a shipment due tonight, sent a couple of our people to scout the area to see if there is anything out of the way, any extra police, etc, etc." Ivan,"OK Boss, will do." He orders three men,"Lets go scout the area anything looks out of sync let us know, now go!" Grumbling the three climb into a Range Rover begin to patrol the neighborhood. One of the Russians was snorting a line of coke looked up just as they were driving past the US Embassy spotted Marjorie and Niran as they exited, he did a double take,"I will be a son of a bitch, that's the broad kicked me in the balls, they are still black and blue. I want a piece of her stop the car." The Driver,"Are you crazy Ivan will have your head if you screw up the drop tonight, she's from the American Embassy."The driver hollered,"Sit the hell down and cool it."He snorted another line and when the Range Rover stopped for pedestrians he starts to open the door to jump out, screaming,"I will kill that witch,I'll rip her head off." The car is a couple of blocks from Marjorie's location, he throws the car door all the way open and takes off running back to where he had seen his prey."

Marjorie had seen his sneering face as the car passed placed him as the Russian she had kicked in the testicles." Grabbing Niran by the arm steered him into the first store she could find,"Follow me we need to exit through the back, don't ask just move I'll explain later."

As they ran to the rear of the store she could hear the crazy Russian screaming I kill the bitch,I kill the bitch!" Once they reached the back of the store Marjorie and Niran turned right heading back to the Embassy. Meanwhile his two companions grabbed hold of their comrade taking him down hard, they grabbed him bodily back to the truck,"You crazy bastard you will get us all killed, you can take her out some other time, now get back in the truck." Marjorie walked back into the Embassy sweating profusely the guard at the door greeting her,"Agent Swift how was lunch?" Marjorie,"Fantastic, absolutely four star couldn't have been better." Embassy Guard,"OH, by the way Agent Morrison is waiting in your office" the guard stated. "Niran I don't need you anymore today, thank you." Morrison, waited till Marjorie entered her office before he greeted her,"Well Agent Swift what has you in a lather or should I say sweat, I got here as soon as possible what the hell is going on?" Marjorie,"We have a problem, there are two in-beds in with the rebels we are hoping to take the entire group down when the arms are delivered, and now I'm being told there's chatter being picked up from this Embassy, I have turned over the auto surveillance section to Johnson and replaced the director we have spies, frigging moles, Jesus this place is awash in bugs, I had to have the furniture in the safe room removed when it was checked the table was bugged.We have a major problem I need your help, badly." Morrison,"I think everyone that works in the Embassy should take a Lie Detector Test. Then we vet every contractor that works for us, unless we make a clean sweep of the Embassy every undercover agent we have in Bangkok will be exposed."

In Thailand when the trawler docked there were two trucks waiting to have the cargo offloaded,"Well at least we don't have to wait, Carl have the crew unload the merchandise and we have to talk, as soon as possible." Carl,"Wait till they're done loading the trucks, then we can talk" Carl answers.

Carl walks into a dense thicket of palms and brush, Henry asks,"What in the hell are you doing?" Carl,"I said we are being watched the CIA has a drone overhead I can feel it in my bones." He opens the briefcase he is carrying and sets a Drone Defense module on the ground. This baby will detect and blind any thing the CIA has surveilling us." Henry,"Where in the hell did you get that?" Carl,"You can thank our Chinese friends they want this mission to succeed as much as we do." Carl activates the Drone Defense System and a drone shows up on the screen, he turns up the ISM band, "Hopefully this System will be able to disable the radio communication they have with their Drone. That will cause their drone to go blind, those CIA pricks can "kiss my fat ass".

Chapter Twenty Eight

"Marjorie we have a problem, the drone surveying the weapons convoy has just gone blind something is interfering with our control platform. Marjorie,"I don't frigging believe Carl and Henry are not involved and not necessarily in that order." Marjorie,"Now, Sammy you'r the expert how can we fix this?" Sammy,"I'll see if I can mute their signal." "Is the drone armed?",Marjorie asks."No, it is not" Sammy answers. Marjorie,"Shit, if they have a predator drone our recon drone is toast, come on people don't just stand there find a solution OK!"

Carl looks at Henry smiling,"Caught the bastards off guard their drone is flying blind hope it crashes into the sea." Carl loads the equipment into the truck smiling." Now lets get to work we'll have to travel at night our people are waiting for us in Thailand. General Hong wants to feed this insurgency to show the Thai government that the Americans aren't as great as they like to think they are.When the rebels are out of control and the CIA cannot stabilize the situation, General Hong will meet with the Thai military and volunteer to defeat the rebels.Of course there will be a caveat that will allow the Chinese Government to build a military base so his government will have a foothold in Thailand rubbing it into the American's noses."

CIA Agent Sammy,"Marjorie, I was able to countermand the frequency now I have control of our drone, the only problem is the drone is running out of power we need to bring it home and recharge the batteries." Marjorie,"What ever, do we have another drone available?" Sammy,"Yes, I'll launch it within the hour." Marjorie,"Good keep me in the loop."

She calls Morrison on her encrypted phone,"Morrison would like you to work with Johnson to set up the Radio Com Section?, I want someone independent of the Embassy to monitor them we need to clean this up once and for all, the moles have to be purged or turned. I would prefer they are erased permanently, we have CIA in-beds that could be exposed this has to be your top priority." Morrison,"I hear you, we are feeding the group false Intel as we speak, there is a satellite monitoring all communications, I should know who the mole is in a couple of days.

It was midnight,Henry and Carl walked around banging on the trucks,"Lets go everybody up! We leave in thirty minutes, we have to be over the boarder by sunrise." The trucks were on the road heading for Thailand, Carl,"When we deliver the goods General Hong has to cough up another two hundred thousand." Henry,"Just watch your back if he doesn't think we are needed he would just as soon snuff us out as pay us." Carl,"You have a point Henry I say we try to collect our cash prior to completing the hand off."

Morrison calls Johnson,"Is the satellite picking up any intelligence?"."Yes, we're picking up an encrypted message it's being intercepted by the Golden Swan"."Good that will allow us to plant a bug and monitor their screen activities, also have a camera bug on the computers in the Embassy so we can monitor the users keyboard and access their passwords." "Johnson don't shut the sting down, we can use this mole to let us tap into their intelligence network with out them knowing."Morrison called Marjorie,"We have our mole it's the Chinese woman we hired six months ago Yu Yan, keep her here I'm going to send a couple of our people to search her apartment, will give you the all clear when we are done." "Read you loud and clear Morrison." Marjorie left her office and watched Yu Yan typing on the keyboard. She saw Marjorie watching her. You Yan stopped typing picked up her purse started for the elevator. Marjorie walked to the elevator touched Yu Yan on the shoulder,"Leaving early Yu Yan, before you leave I have to talk to you." Yu Yan looked startled answering,"Have an emergency have to I go now." Marjorie,"I'll have one of our security drive you home after we talk in my office." She steered Yu Yan into her office. "Sit down we have to talk. There is a mole in the Embassy and I would like you to keep a lookout for anything that looks suspicious." Sitting there with her mouth open she answered,"Yes,I will do as you ask It is my duty." Marjorie replies,"Good keep me in the loop." Marjorie's phone rings she answers,"We are done with the sweep to her apartment, our forensic people have planted bugs in her computer, phone and car" the Agent hangs up.

"Yu Yan, you can leave now, my driver will take you to your apartment" she turned leaving Marjorie's office. Morrison walked into her office shuts the door,"She was vetted till the day she was born, her parents must have been plants in the States and she was raised to be a spy, graduated from Yale, speaks three languages applied for a job at the Defense Department and the Department sent her here to monitor attempted intrusions into the security network, we have been played." Morrison just shook his head.

"Like I said, we use her to give the Chinese Government false information and of course sooner or later they will catch on and knowing General Hong will dispose of her and save us the trouble." Marjorie answers shrugging.

Morrison,"Jesus, You are cold I am glad I'm on your side." "You want to play the game you pay one way or the other, if you get burnt shame on you. I want a tail on that bitch twenty four hours, seven days a week", Marjorie orders.

General Hong,"Have the Golden Swan send up an armed drone and destroy the CIA drone, screw this playing games with the CIA.I want them to know who has the upper hand we will deliver the munitions to the rebels and cause the Thai Government so much trouble they will bend down and kiss my Chinese butt." Crewman,"Captain we have a message from General Hong, they want us to send up an armed drone, intercept and destroy the Capitalist drone to show them they should not be interfering with the mighty power of the Chinese Communist Government." The Captain reacted immediately and called to the Drone Control Pilot on board,"Put in flight our armed drone and destroy the CIA intruder immediately."

Chapter Twenty Nine

The Chinese drone was launched and went immediately into attack mode. Just as the Chinese Drone was about to activate it's machine guns it tilted to the left started free falling to the ground, the Controller fighting with the controls was able to stabilize the drone, but when it righted the drone was only at one hundred feet and crashed into the dense tropical forest exploding in a fire ball. Carl and Henry ducked as the shrapnel from the destroyed Drone shredded the tropical plants like a scythe in a wheat field. They crawled under the truck,"What the frack just happened?" The ammunition from the drone detonated filling the air with the sound of exploding ordnance causing the aftermath of deadly fireworks,"I think General Hong just blew a nut. We have to deliver this cargo to Thailand "ASAP" or we are toast." Carl tells Henry, they crawled from underneath the truck surveying the damage,"the windshield is pitted and the paint job is pocked marked but otherwise the trucks are ready to go." Carl screams at the drivers,"Get your fat butts out of the bush and lets move,I will personally shoot anyone who doesn't get behind the wheel, Now, let's go."

The drivers all climbed into the trucks mumbling something about,"Screw the General." Henry walked out in front of the convoy waving his Uzi,"Anyone has a problem let me know I will settle it here and now, otherwise move." The trucks were started and slowly drove toward Thailand.They crossed the Thai border and one click in Henry motioned for the convoy to pull into a cleared area of palm trees.Carl stayed in his truck monitoring the local chatter,"Henry, everything appears to be clear, our locals are about four clicks out. I would recommend we send out a point team just in case"."Got your sixty brother, everyone keep a sharp eye out and be careful. The rebels advanced on the site with weapons drawn,Carl stepped into the clearing stating,"I need to talk to Abulia now." Abulia,"Carl how are you?" Abulia asks as he steps out into the sunlight,Carl,"We have the weapons as promised, now I need you to keep your part of the bargain payment in gold." Abulia signals to his men and they carry leather bags that jingle,"Here is the gold as promised our Brothers are backing the uprising." Carl,"Henry count the gold and place it in the lead truck." Henry took his time counting the gold,"Yep Carl, it is all here, OK boys, unload the weapons place them in our friends trucks." The weapons were unloaded, everyone stayed on the defensive till the cargo was unloaded and transferred. Henry walked to the front truck looking around opened the door and climbed in started the engine sitting there letting the truck engine idle. Carl,"Was checking with Abulia confirming that everything on the buy list was delivered,"Are we good Abulia any questions?"."All is well my friend."

"OK, we will be on our way, take care see you in the future." Carl walked slowly to the truck and climbed into the passenger side."Henry lets get the Hell out of here.I have a gut feeling something bad is going to happen, real soon." Henry put the truck in gear and drove from the site slowly when they were about a mile away he stomped on the gas, the truck lurched foreword and Henry yelled,"Ya, ho, away we go." The truck didn't stop until they were out of Thailand, there was a loud rumble and a bright flash.

Carl,"Holy Shit the convoy was just bombed,I knew there was something wrong if we had hung around we would have been ashes." General Hong,"Yes." Aide,"There is bad news the shipment of weapons has been vaporized along with most of the rebels."

CHAPTER THIRTY

American Embassy CIA; "How did the mission go?"."Mission complete target obliterated the "DNA" proved we took out the leader of the Rebels, from the chatter General Hong is so pissed off he could chew nails." Agent Johnson shrugs, laughing. Marjorie, "Little did they know we had control of their computers when the Chinese Drone lost altitude crashing into the jungle, I was sure we had finally taken out Henry and Carl, no luck." Agent,"God what a sight." Marjorie,"Anything new on our Chinese mole?"

Johnson,"Yu Yan has been in contact with her handler we followed her to a meet and watched as she passed phone information on our country's military infrastructure.The handler was identified as Mr.Chan he owns a grocery store located in the Oriental Section of Bangkok I have one of our men keeping watch on the store." Marjorie,"It's too bad the drone didn't take out our boys?" Johnson,"No, when we checked the bodies we could not find any of their DNA in the ruins, our man said they took off in one of the trucks about twenty minutes before the drone struck."

General Hong was raving mad,"What idiot allowed the CIA to be able to intercept and use our computers against us?, I will castrate the stupid Son of a Bitch and where in the hell is those two low life scum bags, Carl and Henry?" There was complete silence,"Uh…Uh General they disappeared with the gold, our people found the truck they were driving it has been torched." General Hong,"I want them found that gold is mine, do you understand mine! and… where is the Trawler?"

"Missing Comrade, the crew was found dead on the shore. The only corpses not found were Carl, Henry and the Captain of the Trawler." Henry,"Captain if you are lucky we will let you live, do as I say. I would recommend you take us where we want to go and you will still be breathing ,but you screw with me you will wish you were never born." HENRY smirked as he shoved his Glock into the Captain's mouth. He laughed as the Captain shit his pants the stink ran down his leg leaving a smelly brown stain on his shoes. "Now my friend turn this tub around and head out to sea." Henry,"Carl watch him I'm going to disable the radio." He entered the radio room, the space was loaded with the latest spy ware equipment, drone control, a super computer,"Holy Shit, look at this equipment the Chinese were hacking everybody from the CIA, FBI and Homeland Security and who in the hell else is anybodies guess."

Back at the CIA office,"This should be our pass to get the Chinese off our backs at least for a while.Marjorie thinks,One of her Aides opens her office door,"You have a call on our encrypted line." Marjorie,"Who is it I'm busy as hell?" Agent Johnson, "You won't believe this Marjorie it's our friend Henry." Marjorie,"What's that you say Henry's on the phone? quick lock onto his location, send a drone and waste the bastard" she started to laugh,"Only kidding, what in the hell does he want?" Agent Johnson, "I think you should talk to him first, he has a proposition you may be interested in they have control of a fishing Trawler that is loaded with Chinese Military surveillance gear, encryption equipment and the algorithms to intercept and interpret Chinese Military communications. Henry is willing to turn it over to the CIA if we give him and Carl some breathing room."

"And what if we don't give him breathing room?"Marjorie asks, "He will destroy the equipment and scuttle the Trawler."

"Do we have a fix on the Trawlers location?"."No!."

Marjorie picked up the phone,"Morrison I need to talk to you, we have a major problem, can you step into my office?"

"Be with you in a couple of minutes."Morrison enters Marjorie's office,"What's up?" Marjorie,"Our friends have captured a Trawler loaded with Chinese spy equipment. They want to parley."Morrison just sat with a smile on his face. Marjorie,"What's so damned funny those two are like a permanent migraine." Morrison,"You mean Henry and Carl those two have nine lives, you have to admit their instincts to survive are uncanny. My sense is tell them if we catch them in Thailand or any US territories we will put them away for life, they are probably heading for

India.Have them anchor the Trawler, locate it with a homing device so we can locate it and if what they claim is true they are free to go."Morrison consuls. Johnson is standing at the door listening,"Johnson, tell them we agree to their terms."

Henry calls to Carl,"They agreed to the deal I'll set up the beacon ASAP. We need to get the hell off the boat." Henry thought about dumping the Captain in the ocean but figured when the CIA took the Trawler into tow, he would just be icing on the cake, Henry handcuffed the Captain to the boat rail,"Your lucky I don't dump your slime ass into the drink." Henry knocked him unconscious.

"Lets move Carl, give me a hand loading the gold into the skiff, as soon as the gold was loaded the two set out for Port Blair on the island of Andaman, which was controlled by the Indian Government. Carl asks Henry,"What happens when we get to Port Blair?" Henry,"WE! have reservations at the TSG Grand Hotel for the week. After that who knows I'm sure we will come up with another gig, right brother."He gunned the engine and the skiff headed for the Island.Henry rolled out of bed, pulled the blinds to shield his eyes from the morning sun. Stretched his lean frame feeling more alive as his joints cracked,"AH, GOD it's nice to be in a clean room, clean clothes and no creeping tropical bugs." Walked to the room phone dialed the desk,"Send me a fruit plate, some sweets and coffee in thirty minutes, thank you." He traversed the suite stepped into the shower, letting the warm water cascade over his nude form, soaped up, rinsed, toweled off, stepped into a pair of shorts and tee.There was a knock on the suite door.Henry,"Put the food on the table." The door opens and in walks Carl,"You up already I would think after that "STINKING" boat trip you'd sleep in."

"Carl don't bust my stones, just please shut up and sit. Breakfast is coming and we have to plan our next move.

I say we head to India the CIA would never guess that would be our next stop." Carl,"Where did you hide the gold?" Henry answers,"Don't worry it's in a bank vault in a lock box. It is insured for three million dollars."

There is a knock on the door,"Henry doors not locked."A waiter delivers the food, Henry slips him a twenty, with a bow leaves the room the two men relax, Henry thinks back to their escape from Myanmar.

("The crew of the Trawler were standing on the shore with weapons ready to relive us of our gold, the Captain had put a reward on our heads. As soon as they spotted us started firing I just ran over the son of a bitches there were bodies flying over the hood.I remember the beautiful sound of bones breaking as the truck tires ran over the corpses of those assholes who couldn't get out of their own way. Carl head shot the crew who were still breathing and the only one still using oxygen was the Captain, (because he was hiding on the Trawler")

Later in the day there was a knock on the hotel room door,"Who's there." Courier,"I have your Passports and Visas." "Slide them under the door and let me check them out before you leave." Henry retrieved the Passports and Visas scanned them checked for any flaws,"Looks perfect, how much do I owe you?" He asked with the door still shut." Courier,"The price is five thousand dollars." Henry,"Give me a minute to get the money." He reached into a drawer counted out the five thousand in one hundred dollar bills placed them in a brown envelope then opens the hotel room door slightly handed the payment to the courier,"We are done, you understand?" "Yes Sir." Henry,"Good, now get lost before I change my mind."

"Carl lets get going we have to get to the airport the flight to Delhi leaves in an hour." Carl,"What about our Passports and Visas?" Henry,"Have them in hand, we need to get the hell out of here before the CIA changes their minds and comes looking for us."

Chapter Thirty One

CIA,"Our drone spotted the Trawler it appears that someone is handcuffed to the railing, we have a cutter on the way to take control and bring her in." Marjorie,"How far out is she?" Agent,"At least twenty to thirty six hours to a safe port." Marjorie,"Do we have any ships in the area?"

"A cruiser." Marjorie,"Good, have it meet the Trawler remove the equipment then sink it. I have a gut feeling the Chinese are monitoring us and if they think their equipment will fall into our hands they will sink the Trawler "toot sweet."

Agent Johnson,"Have we been able to spot any foreign drones in the area?" Agent,"None so far." Johnson,"Put a couple of armed drones in the air and keep them over the ship till we can off load all the equipment" Pilot,"Will do." Marjorie looks at Morrison,"All we can do now is wait."

CCU Drone Control,"General Hong our drone still has not found the Trawler"."I don't want to hear your excuses, the equipment on the ship could compromise our intelligence gathering. So we either find it and reclaim the equipment or sink her, don't come back until you have an answer I want to hear, or I will have you shot…DO YOU UNDERSTAND!" The sergeant's knees were shaking as he ran out of the Generals office screaming orders to his men,"Find the ship or I will personally have your heads and if I don't the General will."

General Hong sits back in his chair thinking,"How did those two escape, they must have had a plant in with the Rebels, but how did the plant know our plans, how did the CIA know where the drop was? many, many questions. I will have to cleanse the entire operation and start over.

The High Counsel is very unhappy. I must have the answers before I return to Beijing or my career is over."

India; The plane was landed in Delhi, Carl had already set up a meet with a drug dealer in front of the airport. They deplaned, picked up their baggage and walked outside and waited for a ride. A cab pulled up the rear window opened, "Carl get in and bring your friend." Carl,"Who sent you?" "The boss we're going to his place in the suburbs too many cops around here."The driver opened the passenger door, they climbed into the back seat,"What's the drive time to your bosses place." Driver,"About an hour sit back and enjoy the scenery." Henry,"How do you know this dweeb?" Carl,"I had dealings with him in the States a few years ago, why?"

"I don't know, ever since they put that million dollar bounty on our heads dead or alive I just don't trust anyone.This deal feels like it is going south or maybe I'm just being paranoid.I have a strange feeling that General Hong is setting us up, his job is on the line with the high Council."

CIA Drone,"The Cruiser will make contact with the Trawler at 0600 about fifteen minutes. We have spotted a bogie at about 20,000 feet. I have given instructions to destroy it before it has a chance to impede our removal of the equipment."

General Hong we have found the Trawler it appears the Americans have a Cruiser heading for the Trawler they will make contact in less than ten minutes." Hong,"Connect me to the US Thai Embassy now, that Trawler is under Chinese Government protection." Sergeant,"Yes, Comrade immediately!" "Marjorie you have a call from General Hong, he says if we attempt to remove any equipment from the Trawler or sink it we are breaching international law and he has threatened to fire on our Cruiser." Agent Johnson,"Is there any way we can blind their Drone for maybe half an hour?"Yes Ma'am."Marjorie, "Good, tell the Captain of the Cruiser to send a Team aboard the Trawler, remove the code books and get the hell out of there, OH! Yea, bring whoever is cuffed to the railing."

General Hong calls his Aide,"What is happening I have a feeling they are playing for time, what was the answer from the Embassy?,they said it would be taken under consideration." Hong,"Screw them, and their… consideration destroy the target now." Chinese Pilot,"We have lost visual contact something is interfering with the drone."The controller answers.

CIA,"We received an encrypted message from the Cruiser." [Retrieval complete, do you want the target destroyed?"] Send this message to General Hong and the same to our people,"Trawler is adrift and a menace to navigation it no longer has the right of Innocent passage, we recommend the Chinese Government sink the Trawler." General Hong responds "Send this reply to the CIA." Operator,"The vessel is the property of the Chinese Government you will cease and desist any and all attempts at sabotage of Chinese Government property will be met with force. Any decisions will to be taken by General Hong of the Chinese Government or you will feel the wrath of our military."

Marjorie,"Have our Cruiser leave the area immediately we have what we came for, no use making the General get his balls twisted, is the Trawler Captain talking?" Agent,"Not yet, he claims he doesn't understand english, bring him to the Embassy for questioning per my orders."

General Hong screams,"Sink the Trawler now!" Aide,"Yes General immediately." General Hong,"Who in the hell does the CIA think they are I will lodge a formal complaint with their Embassy in Bangkok for interfering in our internal matters."He sat back pouring himself a glass of Bourbon, with the Trawler destroyed my report will read all sensitive equipment has been eliminated."

Aide,"Mission is complete the Trawler is at the bottom of the ocean." General,"Good, very good, have our drone shadow the Cutter, make sure it doesn't return and try to salvage the equipment." Aide,"Yes Comrade." General there is a call from the "SOF"(Special Operation Forces),"Switch the call to my phone"."Comrade how can I help you?" Head of Bureau,"Are you positive the equipment has been destroyed." General,"Yes we have a video of the Trawler sinking." Head of Bureau,"You are sure the Americans did not remove any equipment from the vessel."

"Absolutely Comrade","I want you to station a patrol boat over the wreck, I am sending a dive crew to salvage the equipment. General Hong I hope for your sake there is nothing missing." "You have my assurances Comrade all the equipment is still on the Trawler." CIA,"What is going on with the Chinese, do we have any intel?"Morrison,"I sent it to CIA Headquarters at Langley, VA. They are decoding it as we speak."

The cab pulled into a dirt road,Henry and Carl glanced at each other with a questioning look, the driver looking in the rearview mirror, laughing,"Keep cool gentlemen the boss has a safe house in the woods where he does his deals." He drove up to the safe house and parked, Henry noticed a sniper sitting in a watch tower, two armed guards were guarding the front of the house, for a hundred yards all the brush and trees had been cleared from around the house.The driver called to one of the guards,"Wand them before you let them in to see the boss." Guard,"No problem Mike."After they were checked out the door to the house opens a tall skinny dude steps out sporting a shoulder holster with a Beretta M9,"Lets go the boss is waiting." They walked slowly up the stairs and into the house, sitting behind the desk was a a bespectacled gentleman, white shirt, tie, very nappy looking,"Mr.Henry and Mr.Carl sit down and let us finish our business deal, I understand you want to buy ten kilos of Cocaine and are looking for someone to supply weapons for terrorists. The cocaine I can furnish, but weapons no, you will have to look to someone else", Anil answers.

Carl,"We can pay in cash for the cocaine just let us know when and where the drop will be"."The price is ten thousand a kilo, Anil,"No problem give me a call, you wouldn't happen to have the cash on hand would you?" Carl,"No way, just set up the drop."

Henry nudges Carl,"We're finished here lets go Carl, the hundred grand will be there for the trade off." The two stood up slowly walked out the front door, the cab was still sitting outside running. They climbed into the backseat and the driver dropped them off on a major highway,"A bus will be here in a few minutes and take you back to the hotel, you will receive a phone call to advise you where to the meet." When the two arrived back at the hotel Henry called the bank,"I need one hundred thousand in hundred dollar bills, Have it ready by morning for pick up."

CHAPTER THIRTY TWO

Russian White Slavers; "The women have been offloaded at the dock, they delivered fifty Uzbeks." Ivan,"Good take them to the farm get them ready we need to start putting them to work, I paid off the local Police Chief he'll look the other way, don't forget when he visits give him anything he wants no charge."

The women were delivered to the farm and taken into the building,"Clean them up, a change of clothes and a meal, tomorrow they start work. You keep your hands off of them, understand Yuri,"Ivan cautioned,"Yes boss, I understand." "Good I would hate to lose a good man."

Ivan's phone rang,"What?" Bodyguard,"You have to come back and listen to this." Ivan,"Listen to what?" Bodyguard,"There is chatter all over the the air waves."

"About what?" Bodyguard,"It seems the Chinese and the CIA have a Mexican standoff over spy equipment.Sounds like the CIA in Bangkok and our friend General Hong are about to come to blows." Ivan,"does this have anything to do with the arms shipment?" Bodyguard,"Hard to tell, we are getting blowback that the shipment was torched right after it was delivered."

"By who?" Bodyguard,"Our source isn't sure, but our ground crew say it appeared to be a (JDAM) from a CIA done." Ivan,"What the hell, what happened to the gold?" he asked. "Gone, the story is our boys Carl and Henry took off with the gold twenty minutes before the explosion." Ivan,"My cut was twenty percent, who in the hell gave Hong permission to give away my percentage?" Ivan fuming dials the General, It rings twice General Hong answers,"Ivan what can I do for you?" Ivan is irate,"What can you do for me? you can pay me the twenty percent I'm owed or I'll come looking for you."

General Hong,"No need to threaten me my friend,Number one I have a thousand troops guarding me, number two those two pains in the ass are working a drug deal as we speak." Ivan looks at the phone trying not to lose it,"And that means what to me?" General Hong,"Look Ivan I am not trying to screw you.I know where they are and what bank the gold has been deposited in, as soon as they take delivery of the cocaine I will take possession of it then turn Carl and Henry over to the CIA you will be paid what you are owed."Ivan,"OK, keep me in the loop and let me know when there will be a meet, Oh by the way who are our friends in India meeting? with our mutual friend Anil?" General Hong hesitated,"Yes, the deal will be done in a couple of days."Ivan hung up thinking,"That son of a bitch is planning to stiff me, screw him and his troops. He's messing with the Russian mafia I will put a price on his head if he tries to screw me out of my percentage of the gold."

CIA;Marjorie called Morrison,"You have a couple of minutes?" "Yea be right in" he opened her office door and threw in his hat,"Is it safe or should I come back?" Marjorie,"Come in Morrison, I want to know what is happening with our mole Yu Yan."

Morrison,"We have her and the old man under surveillance." Marjorie,"What do you know about her physical health, who is her dentist, her doctor, what does she eat for breakfast? I want to know how many times she takes a piss, this Embassy is bugged I just received a "BOLO" on a CIA turncoat a SPY that has been working for us for years the "son of a bitch has sold out our entire crew in China, name Jerry Chun" Marjorie finally stops to take a breath.Morrison,"So you are thinking that our Yu Yan is passing information that this Jerry Chun is feeding her to pass on to ChineseIntelligence." "You got it, see if she needs dental work."Morrison,"What do you have in mind?" Marjorie,"Just find out who her dentist is all you have to do is look at is her dental bills, keep it to yourself." Morrison walks out of the office wondering what in the hell does she have in mind." he walks over to personnel and asks Mable,"Can you bring all the personnel files to my office by noon today?" Mable,"Sure Morrison no trouble." Morrison, "The main office wants me to check a few things." Marjorie's phone rings,"We have a hit on Jerry he just entered the old mans store."

"Don't approach him just keep the store under surveillance. If Yu Yan shows up let me know ASAP." Agent,"Will do boss, I would like to put a bullet in this traitors head." The agents watched as Yu Yan parks in front of the store she sits there a couple of minutes looking around making sure she wasn't being watched. Finally she exits the car entering the store.

"Do you have eyes on the rear of the store?" Agent,"Yes, no one has tried to leave, our thermal imaging shows three people inside." Morrison,"Is there any movement or are the figures stationary?" Agent,"Now that you mention it there hasn't been any movement for the last few minutes."

"Send a couple of our men in and look around I have a feeling the rats have left the sinking ship." The Agents put on their bullet proof vests, checked their Glocks and traversed the distance to the store,"Mack you take the right, I will go left if anyone moves take them out."Talking on his phone","Sammy just stay in the rear in case they try to escape," Sammy,"Roger that."

The store was empty. The Agents when they entered the rear office found three dummies with heat coils keeping them at

98.6 degrees,"We have been played there must be another way out of here, a false door or a tunnel the bastards have given us the slip."

India; The phone in the Suite rings,Henry picks up,"Who is this?" Caller,"Tonight at midnight the meet is at the Kahn Market don't be late"the caller hangs up,"Carl we have the location of the drop, the time is midnight." Henry cautions,"I think we should rent a car just in case we need a fast getaway." Carl calls the desk,"This is Suite 67 we need a fast car at eleven tonight." Hotel Clerk,"Yes Sir, the car will be in front of the hotel at exactly eleven." Harry placed his suitcase on the bed flipped it open lifted his bullet proof vest and put it on,"Carl you better suit up no telling what we will run into."

Henry,"Be there in a sec, I'm wrapping the money will be with you asap."

CHAPTER THIRTY THREE

At eleven the two were standing at the curb a Lincoln SUV pulls up,"Carl, we travel in style"."Lets go, we have a meeting to make."

They arrived a few minutes early,Henry,"Drive around check out the neighborhood." Carl slowed down and coasted through the shopping area,"Look there's two likely perps stand-ing on the corner and there's a sniper on the roof across the street,I say we back off and head back to the hotel.This looks too much like an ambush."Henry," Carl just keep driving straight and when we cross the next street punch it."

Marjorie,"Your daughter is on the phone"."Johnny did she say what she wants?"."Just that she needs to talk to you." "OK, put her on the phone"."Hi Honey, what's going on?"

She was sobbing,"Mom … Mom my friend has been kidnapped, YOU,YOU have to find her, we were walking home and a black van stopped two men dressed in black jumped out and grabbed her, I ran and started screaming for the police.

The two assholes threw Monica in the truck and took off." "Where are you?" Sara,"I'm home, I'm scared MOM, They knew who I was he called me by name." Marjorie,"Did this creep have an accent." Sara,"Yes it sounded Russian." Marjorie,"What did he look like?" Sara,"Big at least six feet tall, probably two hundred fifty pounds, had large hands like base ball mitts." "Did he grab you?" Marjorie asks,Sara is silent for a moment thinking,"He grabbed me and I pulled away, he was left holding my sweater,I started screaming for the police he dropped it then they threw Monica in the van and took off." Marjorie,"Stay where you are two of my Agents will pick you up and bring you to the Embassy for safe keeping, they should be there in half an hour and make sure to bring your sweater I want to have it checked for DNA."

She hung up the phone sitting at her desk thinking, "Russian, big, burly I would bet it's the same son of a bitch I kicked in the balls. He is getting revenge."

Russian Mafia;The van pulled into the garage Monica heard the door close."Get her out of the van lock her in the backroom." "What do we do now, you know Ivan will be totally pissed when he hears about this." Popov,"You keep your mouth shut or they will find you in the river, get my drift!"

"Yes Comrade, understand completely." Popov,"Now, take that bitch and put her in the back room",Popov "SCREAMED" at his partner. He pulled Monica out of the van and dragged her crying to the storage room,"Please, please let me go I won't tell anyone, my mother is sick and this could kill her." "Shut up."he said, Slammed the door and closed the padlocked,"She is driving me nuts, how long do I have to watch her?"."Not long she will be auctioned off tonight."

American Embassy Thailand; Morrison walks in,"We have a fix on Ivan if we want to find Monica he's the man to ask." Marjorie,"Alert the Thai Special Forces, have two of our people accompany them. When they arrest him, bring him to our safe house I do not want that scum bag in the Embassy is that loud and clear." Morrison smiles,"Loud and clear my dear." "Enough smart ass, we need to get Ivan to the safe house before the day is out."

Russian Mafia;"Boss Boris is on the phone You will want to hear what Popov did." Ivan,"put him on the phone what did that moron do now?" Boris,"We are in deep shit, he kidnapped the daughter of an American Diplomat and attempted to kidnap the daughter of the Director of the CIA, she escaped, we are in deep very deep." Ivan,"Tell Popov to put her on the ship I want him in my office immediately."

Ivan,"Where is that moron I will have his head we need to get rid of that girl before the Federals find out"."Ivan we have visitors." Ivan,"Tell them I will see them later" he no sooner answered when his door was kicked off the hinges Thai Troops threw him to the ground, cuffing him,"Lets go Comrade the CIA wants to see you about an attempted kidnapping and a missing teenager." Ivan,"I have no idea what you are talking about? I run a legit business."

CIA Safe House; Agent Johnson,"You deal in white slavery, drugs and weapons, where is the other girl?"

Ivan,"I don't know anything about some missing broad."

"Her name is Monica and the girl who escaped is the daughter of a CIA officer, let's go!"

The Thai Special Forces manhandled Ivan into the Police Car. They drove to the safe house turned him over to the CIA Agents,"He's all yours I hope when you clear this up, then turn him over to us." The Thai Lieutenant quipped. The Agents placed him in a holding cell cuffed his hands to the steel bar welded to the table that was bolted to the floor. Marjorie muscles were tensed like a Cobra ready to strike as she stood looking through the two way glass separating her from Ivan.

Morrison tapped her on the shoulder,"You look like you want to kill, relax your turn will come." Marjorie opened the door to the Interrogation Room slowly walked to the table stood staring at Ivan. Marjorie,"That creep Popov that works for you kidnapped the daughter of one of our Embassy personnel and tried to take my daughter. We get her back I will drop all charges or I will make your life so fucking miserable your bosses in Moscow will take you out themselves… and I want Popov thats the deal."

Ivan just sat there,"I have no idea what you are talking about" he answered. Marjorie,"I will give you fifteen minutes then the Thai Police will begin closing down your operations." Marjorie started to peel off addresses," grow houses, brothels and halfway houses." Opened her phone and started dialing. "OK,OK we have her at the Garage on the circle that stupid Popov was looking to revenge your crushing his balls."

"When I get done with him he'll be lucky if he isn't castrated" Marjorie quips.She calls Morrison,"Monica is at Ivan's garage it's located at the circle, go take that bastard down I will wait here, because if I go Popov will never leave alive." Morrison,"I read you Marjorie keep Ivan there till we clear this up."

The Thai Special Forces surrounded the Garage and deploy ready for a fire fight, the Lieutenant gives the signal to take down the door. Two of the soldiers picked up the battering-ram with one shot take out the door, it flew across the floor of the garage and landed with a loud "CRACK". The troops filtered into the space,"Lieutenant the place is empty." Lieutenant,"Check the back and if you find anything let me know immediately." His Sergeant calls out,"All clear but there are signs that someone was being kept prisoner in a cage at the back of the building."

CHAPTER THIRTY FOUR

The Lieutenant called,"Johnson why don't you and your men see if you can find any prints or maybe a clue as to where they took her." Johnson,"Sounds good."

Johnson went through papers laying on the desk and spotted a shipping invoice for a crate to be loaded on a ship that was leaving the local port in less than twenty four hours. He flipped his phone open,"Marjorie they have her on a cargo ship the Madeas you have to stop it from leaving port the girl is being held there." Marjorie,"Are you sure?"

"I would bet my badge on it they are taking her out of the country, if that happens we will never see her again." Marjorie,"I will leave immediately, you the Lieutenant and his men head for the ship,NOW!" The entire crew left with screeching tires for the Madeas. The gang way was being rolled up when they arrived, Johnson drove up to the ship jumped out and pulled his gun,"STOP, I'm the police we have to search the ship",the stevedore hollered back,"Go screw, we are casting off now." Johnson cocked his pistol and fired over the stevedores head.

"I said stop moron or the next one will be in your head, now back up we are boarding the ship." They rushed the gang way and all of sudden there was a burst of gun fire from a machine gun, the bullets were pinging and ripping the wooden walkway throwing splinters,"Stay where you are" the gun man hollered,"or the next burst will be the last." Johnson signaled to the Lieutenant running his finger over his throat signaling take him out, the Lieutenant gave his star sniper the thumbs up and there was a sharp"BANG" the gunman straightened up with a very surprised look collapsing face down spurting blood on the ships deck.

"One down maybe a few more to go, don't stand there take the ship and anyone you see armed take them out, don't give the bastards a chance to shoot." They started to search the ship inch by inch. The rest of the ships crew was taken into custody and questioned, finally the second mate asked to speak to Johnson out of earshot of the others,"There is a false bulkhead on the lower deck where they have hidden thirty girls to be sold into slavery." Agent Johnson,"Show me where the bulkhead is and how it can be breached."

"You will need a couple men and a torch they welded it closed the women have food and water to last for the length of the voyage."

Agent Johnson ran back into the holding room,"Lieutenant grab a couple of the crew have them bring a torch follow me to the lower deck, there are women being held prisoner below, let's move this ship is being (quarantined)."

When they reached the lower deck the second mate guided them to the false bulkhead,"See these welds cut them top and bottom, but before you do that rig a winch so the weight of the plate doesn't kill some body."

The acrid smoke from the welding was more than they could stand,"bring a couple of fans to clear out the smell we don't want to asphyxiate anybody.The plate was winched out of the way and inside a stinking hole not fit for pigs were crammed the women,"Do you believe this shit they make the women piss in buckets and pour it out the port hole that is criminal, we need to find that White Slaver and turn him over to Marjorie she will have him crying like a baby" everybody started laughing,"you got that right" one of the Agents wisecracked.

They led the young girls out of the sewer and took their names. Johnny pulled Monica aside,"When we leave the ship your parents are waiting for you on the dock" she started to cry,"They said I was going to be one of their whores I was real scared Mr.Johnson I saw them do things to some of the girls they cried." Johnson,"Your OK, now sweetheart we'll get those slavers and put them away for a long, long time."

Marjorie was standing at the bottom of the gangway, wondering,"If it wasn't for the All Points Bulletin to find the people who had kidnapped Monica and free her these girls would be God knows where and sold into "WHITE SLAVERY". The girls were helped off by the Thai Police and ushered into a waiting bus, watching the relief and smiles on their faces brought tears to Marjorie's eyes, she turned away when she saw Morrison giving her the look,"I must Never, Never let anyone see me show any weakness." She hollered to Johnson,"Make sure they all have a hot shower and a change of clothes." Johnson,"Will do boss all is good." Monica crawls into the Embassy SUV hugging her mother and father. Marjorie thinks,"Now,I have to find Popov, he needs to be put away for at least fifty years of hard labor."

Ivan,"Popov what in the hell were you thinking, kidnapping that girl has the US government, the Thai Government and every Goddamned agency in the world is on my ass. If I don't turn you over to the CIA my operation is trashed."

Chapter Thirty Five

"That bitches mother kicked me in the balls, I couldn't let some woman make me look like a fool I had to make her pay." Popov retorted. Ivan just sat there looking at Popov.

"You have the brains of frigging ape, I can't afford to have the CIA question you, you know too much." Ivan picked up his pistol cocked it pointing it at Popov's head.

Two of Ivan's men walked into the office,"What do you want us to do with him boss?" Ivan,"Take him to the Crematorium and give him his last rites, then dump his ashes in the river." Popov,"Jesus Christ, boss, PLEASE, I WON'T TELL THEM ANYTHING!" Ivan just waived,"Get this moron out of my sight and take care of business."They took Popov to the floor tying his hands and feet, dragged him to the loading dock dumped him into the trunk of the car,"Don't stand there you drive, I'll ride shotgun." They climbed into the car and drove to the Crematorium. They could hear Popov thrashing around in the trunk,"Be careful when you open the trunk that bastard is as strong as a bull, the driver picked up a crowbar from the back seat,"Maybe if I break a few bones the creep will shut up and calm down, I never did like him. Always starting trouble and throwing his weight around,"He pushed the button and watched as the trunk slowly opened, Yury raised the crowbar and brought it down on Popov's head there was a loud crack and blood sprayed from the wound on Yuri's shirt. He raised it to finish the job and Michael grabbed his arm,"STOP, if you kill him we will have a hell of a time getting him in the coffin, let's move him while he's still groggy.They pulled Popov out of the trunk and dragged him into the Crematorium, Popov was thrashing around the two men were having a hard time controlling him,"Give him a shot of Heroin that should calm him down." Michael jammed the needle in his neck and watched as Popov went limp,"Ok, help me put this elephant in the coffin, they placed the limp, barely breathing body in the coffin, nailed the lid closed. Mike,"We have to wait till the furnace reaches 1400 degrees, then start the rollers, by the time were are done he will be a pile of dust, activated the rollers that would take the coffin into the blazing furnace. The coffin started to rock violently the coffin lid flew off landing on Michael knocking him to the concrete floor. The sides exploded as Popov crashed out of the coffin sending splinters flying. Yuri went for his gun Popov landed on him and planted a hidden knife into his left eye,"You won't be using that crowbar again,"There was a scream of pain"AAAAA,H" as Yuri started to convulse, Popov just laughed and drove the knife deeper into his brain the body twitched a couple of times Yuri lay still. Popov picked up Yuri's body and threw it on the rollers and pushed the button watching as his body was slowly consumed by the flames. Meanwhile Michael was recovering from being hit on the head by the lid of the coffin, he watched in silence as his partner was consumed in the flames, with the body moaning and twisting till there was nothing left but ashes.

He pulled his Glock and fired it at Popov , the first slug caught Popov in the shoulder, the second shot missed Popov screamed like a wild man ran crashing out the Crematorium door escaping into the street."I'll be a son of a bitch that Popov is like the "HULK, I better call Ivan and let him know Popov is alive and looking for revenge." Ivan's phone rang,"Hello, what do you want Michael?" Michael,"He's escaped." Ivan,"Who escaped? what in the hell are you talking about?"

"It's Popov that crazy bastard killed Yuri and burned his body I put a slug in his shoulder but he escaped he's probably coming for you boss."

Ivan put down his phone called to his secretary,"Tell the crew I want everyone in my office immediately."

"Yes sir I'll tell them now." The crew crowded into the office,Ivan,"Our boy Popov has escaped and is probably coming for vengeance everyone needs to stay awake he will off anyone of us without even blinking, so If he's seen, shoot to kill." Bang, Bang,"Open up Dao, Dao hurry up I'm shot!"

The door opens and Popov falls into her arms slowly sliding onto the floor,"What happened my love I'll call the police" he laid there bleeding on the floor,"Don't call the police, don't call anyone have your brother see what he can do, he's studying medicine. If they find me I'm a dead man." Popov opened his eyes, trying to roll over every bone in his body screamed pain, his shoulder was bandaged and he was on an "IV". He slowly pulled out the IV rolling out of bed, put on his pants and shirt, stumbled to the closet and pulled out the Uzi gabbed as many clips he could jam in his pockets, mumbling to himself,"They have to pay, Povov needs to get even, nobody screws with Popov… I kill Ivan first then that bitch… from the CIA and anybody that gets in my way." He lurched out the door and down the street. "Marjorie!,the Thai police put out a Bolo for Popov, he just hijacked a truck and is heading for Ivan's office." His girlfriend called the police said he's armed with a Uzi and is planning to take out Ivan and anyone else who gets in his way."Marjorie,"Send a crew to the Russians hideout, maybe we can capture Popov before the police or his former gang members put a bullet in his head." The Thai Police surrounded the Russian's base of operations waiting for the arrival of Popov. Morrison and Johnson pulled up to the Thai Police van and exited walking toward Lieutenant Kiet,"Lieutenant any sign of Popov and what's happening inside." Kiet,"We confiscated their weapons and placed six men just in case that crazy bastard gets inside, as for Popov the truck he stole was found a couple of blocks from here bloody bandages on the seat abandoned."

Morrison looks at the Lieutenant asking,"We would like to take him alive I am sure we can squeeze intel out of him that would be helpful to everyone involved."

Morrison asked,"How familiar are you with the Chinese government dealing in human organs, there is mucho scuttlebutt concerning the scenario of China harvesting human organs from religious prisoners." Lieutenant,"The Russians have been dealing with the Chinese and sending their upper level people that need transplants to China for the operation." Morrison and Johnson speak in unison,"What in the hell aren't the Russians into?"

Lieutenant Kiet laughs answering,"Anything and everything we think they are being bankrolled by the Russian FSB, as you know they are always looking for new revenue streams."

There was a screech of tires and a SUV careened around the street corner on two wheels heading straight for the building. The Lieutenant hollered,"Get out of the way he's going straight for the front wall." The Thai Police raised their pistols to fire, all of a sudden there was a loud BOOM and before the Thai Police could shoot there was a second BOOM and the car swerved to the right Popov tried to control the vehicle but it continued to careen, flipping over and over coming to a screeching halt, landing on it's roof. The weight of the car blew the glass Popov was knocked senseless with a concussion,"Get him out of the car before it blows.There's gas leaking everywhere."

Johnson cautions. The Thai Police drag him out of the car and cuff him. The Lieutenant,"You want us to take him to your Embassy?" Morrison answers,"Take him to the back of the compound and we will take him from there. Popov was hauled into the police van and the CIA Agents followed them to the Embassy,"There is a Thai Police Van heading to the Embassy when it arrives let them enter we are right behind it."Morrison called ahead warning the Embassy guards.

The Police Van entered the Embassy and stopped to remove the prisoner.Marjorie was waiting impatiently in the court yard.The police removed Popov Marjorie walked up to him and stuck Popov with a syringe in the juggler.He went totally limp."Put him on the gurney wheel him in put his dead ass in a basement cell. Watch the bastard he is as strong as an ox and dangerous even when he's comatose."

They took him into the cell/interview room he was seated on a steel chair anchored to the floor, cuffed him to a stainless steel bar they left waiting for Popov to wake up. Marjorie watched through the two way mirror waiting for any sign of Popov stirring. He groaned when he tried to raise his cuffed hands "BELLOWED" when he realized he was hogtied. Rose up and attempted to lift the steel table that was anchored to the concrete floor with so much force that one of the anchors ripped out of the concrete.

"Jesus that guy is a gorilla,"Marjorie laughs,"Send in a couple men to calm that crazy bastard down before he wrecks the Embassy." Four guards entered the cell with shields and stun guns to subdue Popov after three shocks he collapses on the floor."What do you want us to do with him?"

CHAPTER THIRTY SIX

Marjorie ponders,"Take him to Solitary and turn off the lights, I want a twenty four hour watch on Popov take his belt and anything he can hang himself with." Guard,"You got it Ma'am." Marjorie,"OH, by the way give him a shot to make sure he doesn't wake up."They strapped Popov on a gurney transported him into solitary and left him in a drugged fog. "What now Marjorie?,we have seven days a week surveillance on the Russian mafia hangout, the story on the street is they have a hundred kilo of heroin being delivered some time this week, the Thai police have a tail on Ivan and his first lieutenant." Marjorie,"Wake up Popov I want to interrogate him in his cell." Guard,"I'll clean him up give me half hour."

Marjorie's phone rings,"Hello!" Guard,"He's all set we anchored him to the frigging wall." She walked to the cell and peered in,"Popov you ready to talk?" Popov,"Go screw bitch when I get out of here I will… kill you!" Marjorie,"We have enough on you to put you away for twenty years in a Thai prison, we have you for kidnapping the daughter of an American diplomat, white slavery, drug running you name it moron the list goes on and on." He started to tremble realizing that he was in deep shit. Popov,"Look I need a deal."

"She turned on the tape recorder,"Start talking, we know there is a drug drop scheduled for sometime this week, when and where?"

Popov,"I don't know exactly where, but the drugs are coming in this Friday, they normally use a boat to deliver them." Marjorie,"You know Ivan has put a price on you alive or dead preferably dead, give me good intel and I will incarcerate you in a Federal Prison in the States and when you serve your time they will give you a new identity." Popov starts to talk,"Ivan has cut a deal with General Hong of the Chinese Special

Forces, they are dealing in harvested organs, drugs, weapons and white slavery." Marjorie thinks, "Everything goes back to this General Hong, it seems the intel we have that China will do anything to to enrich the country's treasury, is correct."

Morrison calls Marjorie,"What now? our boys in India have dropped off the radar,Carl and Henry are no where to be found." Marjorie,"We had two of our people following them they were supposed to pick up a few kilos of coke"

Morrison,"They never showed up they have nine lives, probably smelled a rat and decided to drop out of sight."

Marjorie thinking to herself,"I have to get a handle on those two before they start a Turf war between the Chinese and Russians."

India; Carl,"Henry what did you do with the gold?" Henry,"Exchanged it for Bearer Bonds and overnighted them to a Bank in the Caymans that way they can't follow the money on my computer."

Carl,"Cool where do we go from here?"

"I say we pit the Russians against the Chinese they have been trying to set us up, to take back the gold, then take us out with violent prejudice."

Carl,"What do you have in mind?" Henry,"We set our boy Ivan up to take a fall. How's your Chinese Carl?"Henry asks.

"My Mandarin is up to par." Henry,"You call our General Hong to set up a weapons sale with the Russian's, we ambush the Chinese before they can deliver then leave evidence that they were double crossed by Ivan and his boys."

"How in the hell are we going to do that?" Henry,"We hire a crew don't let them know what the target is, the crew will be expendable if they get wise they just disappear. We sell the weapons to the rebels that will give us a nice stash to start over."Ivan there's a call from General Hong,"Hello General what can I do for you?" Carl,"I just received a shipment of weapons and I need somebody to set up a delivery, are you in?"

Carl,"Hell yes! It will cost you half a million plus the cost for delivery." Hong,"Half a million no cost for the delivery." The speaker on the other end counters. Ivan,"It's a deal when and where." Carl,"This Saturday I'll let you know the time and place. No more communication till the meet. The CIA is monitoring all chatter."Carl ends the conversation.

"Ok, now it's your turn Henry",Henry dials his phone it, rings twice," General Hong's desk"."This is Ivan I need to talk to the General"."General someone named Ivan wants to talk to you"."Give me the phone, what's up Ivan?"."One of my clients needs a couple million in weapons all heavy goods if you get my drift" General Hong,"There is a convoy on the way, it can be transferred in Cambodia and your people can deliver it to the rebels in Thailand",the General answers,"The deal will cost you half a million in American dollars I know that the Chinese government does not want to be tagged so the price is more than fair."

American Embassy CIA; Marjorie,"Have we been able to find the "BOBBSY" twins?" Johnson,"Not yet Marjorie we have every Agency looking for them Carl and Henry are still missing."

"I have a strange feeling something is going down, but I still haven't figured what."

Marjorie grimaced,"Johnson send up a couple of drones I want surveillance on General Hong and the Russian enclave twenty four hours till I say other wise" Johnson,"Will do and by the way we have eyes on our spy Yu Yan she has taken refuge at the Chinese Embassy. Any sight of the old man or the other mole?" Marjorie asks,"They seem to have disappeared from the face of the earth. My guess they crossed the border into Cambodia and are looking for a pickup by our friend General Hong, in other words long gone."Johnson answers,"Let me know if there is any movement from the Chinese camp"."Will do boss."

Carl dials General Hong's headquarters(speaking Mandarin)"I need to talk to the General,General Hong how are you?"Ivan, "Great when and where the meet?"

HOng,"Saturday at the Cambodian border the guards have been bribed to look the other way. There will be three, two ton trucks loaded with weapons and the half a million in dollars will be delivered in hundred dollar bills."

"Same place same time?"."Yes the same place as usual." "Good, very good my people will be there at daybreak." Carl acting as Ivan hung up the phone

Chapter Thirty Seven

Henry,"Are we all set?" Carl,"Yes we'll need a dozen men to pull this off." Henry,"I contacted my old gang and offered them double the usual take and they jumped at it." Saturday they loaded the SUV's with grenades and Uzis,"We need to be at the meet a couple of hours early to set up." They set up the machine gun twenty yards from the border, the Border Guards had abandoned their posts were drinking five clicks down the road at a local hooch.

"They should be here in about an hour four vehicles just like they said." Carl,"Leave the drone active till we contact the Chinese convoy,I want to make sure they aren't wise to us and this is a set up"."Henry the delivery is right on time" "Have our people get out of sight,Carl you negotiate the transfer." The crew faded back into the brush and waited just incase there was a problem. The Chinese convoy stopped a few yards just short of the border and waited.Carl walked from the underbrush approached the first truck addressing the lead driver in "Mandarin",Ivan sent me. I have trucks hidden in the palm grove just in case the CIA has a drone surveilling the border." The convoy pulled into the thicket unloading the weapons.Carl,"Where's the half a million?" Lieutenant,

"It's in the back of the truck." Carl,"I need to count it before I leave to make sure the General didn't short me" the blood drained out of the Chinese Lieutenant's face,"I... think you should wait till we leave, my orders are to leave as soon as the weapons are offloaded."

"Hey, Henry do me a favor(speaking in english)I think the Lieutenant is looking to screw us out of the half a million. Alert our men and why don't you follow me to the back of his truck while I count the pay off."

Henry picked up an Uzi from the seat of the truck and followed Carl to the back of the Lieutenants Jeep."

Carl tells the Lieutenant,"Lets get this over with do me a favor and open the suitcase. I want to count the money before we go anywhere." Henry stood with his back to the truck the Uzi locked and loaded. He noticed the other soldiers were looking nervous, he whispered to Carl,"I think these assholes are looking to take us out, they are just waiting for us to show weakness and POW we are… dead." Carl has a pistol under his coat, he pulls it and jabs the pistol in the Lieutenant's ribs,"Just gently pick up the bag carry it to the SUV very slowly place it in the back seat then walk away or you are a dead man." The Lieutenant did as he was told and after leaving the money walked slowly back to his truck climbing into the drivers seat, he just sat in the jeep staring out the windshield.

Carl,"I think he's going to make a move but hasn't figured out what is a good time to take us"."I say we act first, we have the weapons and the half a million. I'll warn our people to keep alert I can feel the animosity from here. They will kill to get their piece of the pie."

The Chinese Lieutenant speed dials the main base,"I need to talk to the General ASAP."Aide,"General, Lieutenant on phone." "What he want? just take care of those two creeps and bring me their heads." Aide,"General says take care of business. Lieutenant answers,"We are surrounded by a half a dozen men with automatic weapons they took the money."There was silence on the other end. Henry watches as the Lieutenant starts to sweat he takes out a rag and wipes salty rivulets from his eyes, the Lieutenants hand is shaking like he has palsy. Henry looks at Carl and they start to laugh. Henry,"Look Comrade I don't know what to tell you, we have your balls between two stones, you have one minute to make up your mind, understand?"

CIA; "Marjorie our drone has picked up movement near the Thai/ Cambodian border, There is a convoy of trucks and it appears they are off loading weapons, the trucks have Chinese Military markings, we can't make out who the other people are." Marjorie,"Put the camera on the big screen and zoom in on the other crew", the camera on the Drone was repositioned,"Bring it in closer see if we can identify whoever is leaning on the back of the truck."

The drone's camera magnifies the picture and Majorie says, "I'll be a son of a bitch that's Henry and I'll bet Carl is the figure standing next to him. Do we have any people close by?, now is our chance to grab and bag those two." Morrison answers,"Every one of our assets is at least one hundred clicks out, and even if we could snag them we are outgunned three to one."

"Henry, we have to wrap this up and scoot I have a feeling we are being watched. It wouldn't surprise me if the CIA has a drone surveying us." Carl explains looking worried. "What do we do with General Hong's boys?"Carl asks. Henry, "Give them a choice drop the weapons or we kill them."

Carl speaks in Mandarin,"Drop your weapons, leave or die, do it now I won't ask again." They watched as the Lieutenant un- holstered his pistol and placed the barrel to his temple and pulled the trigger, his brains blew all over his Sergeant who promptly puked,"Jesus, what was that all about?"Carl,"He lost face so he took his own life to protect his family." The rest of the troops dropped their weapons climbed into the trucks, turned them around quietly drove away."Well at least we didn't have to slaughter them." Henry,"OK, lets get the hell out of here."Follow our truck across into Thailand there is a warehouse a few klicks over the border, I will let you know what to do when we get there. Carl,"I will bet that drone is sitting up there the "CIA eye in the sky" our friend Marjorie is salivating to get her hands on us, it makes her all hot and bothered."

"We have to dump the weapons and screw I would guarantee they have assets coming our way as we speak."

Marjorie asks"Where are our people?" Agent,"Just a few minutes Marjorie they will be on site." Marjorie,"Tell them to be cautious, knowing those two.This grab is way too easy."She watched the screen as the Agents spread out approaching the warehouse.Marjorie,"Is there any movement?" Johnson,"So far nothing."Johnson have your people place a charge on the main door and set the timer."Everyone take cover!" there was a loud explosion as the door blew inward, Agents stormed the building."The building is empty, the trucks are still here, but no weapons and our two perps are missing."

Henry,"We screwed out of there just in time, our next stop is the safe house. The General is probably raving mad. I can see him foaming at the mouth like a RABID dog."Carl,"We need to turn this half million into bearer bonds and deposit it in the Caymans right away."

Ivan,"I wonder if the General was able to take out Carl and Henry, those two morons thought they could scam me and the General, they have another think coming." Bruno,"Hey boss the General is on the line and he is pissed off." Ivan takes the phone,"What's up Hong?" General,"Don't Hong me, those two ambushed my men stole you're half million, took the weapons then disappeared. I need you to track them down kill them." Ivan,"You are shitting me, they bogarted the coin and the weapons?, how in the hell did they pull that off?" General Hong,"I have no frigging idea, they one upped me. I will give those two are as slippery as eels. Ivan, please, please … make their deaths VERY, VERY painful I want my weapons back."

Chapter Thirty Eight

CIA:"Is our spy still hiding in the Chinese Embassy?" "Yea, we have a twenty four hour watch no movement. Do you think we can find a reason for her to want to leave the Embassy?" Marjorie,"Think about it maybe she has family we can use as leverage, check it out." Johnson answers,"You will be kept in the loop." Marjorie walks into her office, closes the door reached into her desk drawer pulls out a bottle of bourbon fills a glass half full and sits there sipping the BURBON, thinking," I need some time off I think I'll take a vacation with my daughter. France sounds good I need to get the hell away, far, far away."

Ivan calls in his Lieutenant,"We have to catch those two they screwed me out of a million dollars in weapons and dollars. Put the word on the street there's a million dollar reward for Carl the same for Henry dead or alive, in order to collect they have to bring me their heads."

"Yes boss, I will put the word out on the street the reward should give us instant results."

Henry,"What's going on?" Chan,"Boss the weapons are gone the men guarding the warehouse are dead." Henry,"Who in the hell did this." Chan,"It looks like the Russians, I found this flyer It has your picture and Carls they have a million dollar reward on your heads dead or alive. It's from Ivan Petrov of the Russian Mafia, he left a note pinned to one of the bodies." Henry,"What does it read?" Chan,"When he catches you he will enjoy cutting you up while you are still breathing then put your head on a pole and carry it around for a trophy."

"Boss I think he is really…,really… mad at you."

Henry tells Borey,"Bring in the rest of the men we can't let the Ruskes screw over us." The blood drains out of Borey's face,"No can do boss the rest of crew shit pants and run away. They afraid of Russian Mafia." Henry doesn't say a word thinking,"We are in a world of hurt, he phones Carl it rings three times,"What in the hell do you want?, I was just getting ready for a good lay." Henry,"Carl we have a major problem I need to see you now!" Carl,"I said I am getting… there was silence….Henry,"What the HELL is going on?" Carl whats happening, "This crazy bitch said she's going to kill me and collect a million American dollars." Henry drops the phone and asks Borey,"Where in the hell is Carl?"."He in whore house across street.", Henry picks up the phone,"Tell her I'm on the way over with two hundred thousand". He grabbed an Uzi out of the SUV made sure the clip was full and dashed across the street, kicked open the Bordello door."What room is Carl in?,speak now or you are a dead man." The clerk pointed to the third door down the hall" as Henry passed the desk he spotted the clerk reach under the counter and saw the glimmer of a pistol.

Without thinking he spun around spraying the clerk with a burst of gun fire, the first struck him in the left torso spinning him so his back was to Henry the second burst took off the top of his head BLOOD spurted against the large mirror in back of the counter and the corpse collapsed on the floor.Henry ran down the hall and knocked on the door,"Carl let me in I have the money",he could hear Carl,"Look I told you he would bring the money, just put the gun down let me open the door." The woman answered,"You better not screw with me or I kill both of you." Henry called to Carl,"Get on your knees and pray when you let me in." Carl,"GOT IT BROTHER, will do." Henry swung the door open and dived for the floor. She turned firing at Henry, without hesitating he fired a burst BANG,BANG,BANG she had a look of complete surprise on her face and as the gun dropped from her hand fell face forward her face smashed on the tile floor.Henry smiled as her life blood spread like the tide across the room,"Damn glad I don't have to clean this stinking mess up.Lets go Carl don't just stand there she was going to shoot both of us, half of Thailand is looking to collect the bounty on our heads, including the dead desk clerk."

Borey bowed to Henry,"Not me boss I stay loyal." Henry,"Ok,OK, Borey just walk in front not me. I don't trust anybody." Before crossing the street Carl made sure the coast was clear,"Looks good Henry we need to make a run for it. They crossed the street and ran back into the building.

Carl,"What the hell is going on." Henry,"We have a price on our heads our friend Ivan is pissed, we screwed him out of a cool million, he started laughing I haven't seen anybody this mad, since I PISSED in General Hung's tea pot."

Carl laughing,"Henry you have one weird sense of humor." "Hey where's Borey?" Carl,"I thought he followed us when we left the Bordello." Henry that weasel is going to drop the dime on us. I'll bet he's on the phone as we speak giving Ivan our location, we have to move."

There was the screech of tires and a SUV traveling at high speed jumped the curb two men opened up with machine guns. Within seconds the windows in the building were blown out, shards of glass flew across the room embedded in the rear wall.The two crawled across the floor,"There's a trap door in the floor wait till they stop firing and go for it, the torrent of bullets stopped for a few seconds.

Henry,"NOW,NOW move your fat ass Carl or we are dead men." The hatch was flung open Carl went first and Henry fell on top of him pulling the door shut."Quick move it, go straight down the tunnel till you see daylight." The SUV backed up crashing through the front wall with machine guns blazing. The car stopped the killers jumped out guns ready."Where did they go?"

The SUV stopped over the escape hatch, they opened up with the machine guns and blew out the back wall.

Chapter Thirty Nine

Carl crawled out of the storm drain,"Jesus Christ, nothing like crawling through a pile of shit." Henry,"Carl shut up and move over quit whining."The two fugitives crawled along a berm. Carl,"What Henry?, you smell worse than a hog pen. The Russians can find us by the odor of our perfume of shit, we have everyone from General Hong, the Russians,Thai Rebels, a drug dealer from Vietnam and who in the hell else is anybody's guess. I have been trying to figure out which way we should turn." Carl,"If we ever get out of this alive, believe it or not I think we should seek asylum at the US Embassy." Henry,"WHAT!!are you nuts?they are looking to put us away for life or longer." Carl,"At least we would still be breathing.

Look if we get them to relocate us to the states, maybe we could get bail and disappear into the woodwork. Maybe start another gig in South America." Henry just stood there looking at Carl,"OK! Brother how in the hell are we going to make it to the Embassy without being snuffed out?"

Ivan,"What do you mean they disappeared?" Boris,"Boss that building looked like Swiss cheese they just vanished."

"Put out a BOLO and up the reward to two million we have to get a handle on where they are, General Hong is ripping. We have the weapons but the money is gone and we haven't been able to trace it. I want you to find what's left of his crew and bring them here so we can question them maybe we can get one of them to give them up." The Russians spread out,"I have a list of their men and addresses, each of us should take three or four of them see if we can get any info out of them. They finally tracked down two of Henry's crew."I don't know anything Henry owes me money believe me if I knew where he was I would give him up in a heartbeat." Sergi,"Ivan wants to talk to you, just talk,OK."

Borey,"Hell NO, you want to talk to me It will be here screw you, this is my turf." Sergi,"Look asshole I said you are coming with me." Borey,"Look around you Russian screw these are my people you put a hand on me and your boss won't be able to recognize you."

Sergei looked around and there were a dozen men standing around all armed with weapons."So back off I don't know where either of them are." Sergi,"OK,OK, no problem but do me a favor if you hear anything let me know and there's a reward for any info and two million if you bring them in dead." "I'll keep that in mind, see you later."

Carl,"How far is the Embassy?" Henry,"it's clear across the city. I have to find a phone maybe I can cut a deal with Marjorie and the CIA can take us into custody. That is the only way we will survive, there are a million Thais out there looking to literally take our heads."

"Marjorie, you have a phone call I think you may be interested in what they have to say." Marjorie,"Look, I'm leaving for Paris in a couple of hours give it to Morrison or Johnson."

"Marjorie it's Carl and Harry they want to turn themselves in will only surrender if you bring them in yourself."

"Are you damned kidding they wait till I'm going on vacation then decide to give themselves up.Johnson will you please put a hold on my flight call my daughter and let her know",Marjorie sighs exasperated,"Vacation, who needs a Vacation",Tell Morrison to assemble the crew and get their location, the word on the street is Carl and Henry have a price on their heads. The Russian Mafia wants them dead and also our infamous General Hong wants what is left after Ivan is done."

Morrison,"I called the Thai Special Forces Lieutenant Sunan just arrived with two armored HUMVEE'S and eight troopers, Johnson is driving the bullet proof SUV. Carl and Henry are about an hours drive from the Embassy, our drone shows them surrounded by the Russian Mafia, this has turned into a turf war between the Local Drug Dealers, the Russians, Carl and Henry are in the middle with General Hong waving his baton leading the parade,"Marjorie,"We need those two alive and kicking. It will be a feather in our caps and probably promotions if we can take them alive and have them stand trial in the States."

Henry, watched as the Russies went from house to house making sure Carl and Henry weren't being protected by the locals. When the block was cleared they moved across the street closer next to the building they were hiding in,"Carl they are slowly choking us off, we are trapped like rats in a sinking ship." Carl snarls,"Screw them I don't know about you I'm not going down without a fight, he drew his Glock, loaded a clip taking protection behind a steel column.

Henry breaths slowly saying,"Hopefully the CIA will get here before the Russians kill us." Carl laughs,"We sure have our selves in a mess, everyone has us on their hit list." Marjorie,"How much longer?" Agent,"About half an hour, our in- bed says the Russians have the Drug Dealers on the run and they are closing in on Henry and Carl.Ivan literally wants their heads, he needs them to collect the bounty from General Hong." Ivan called his Lieutenant,"Where are they?"

"They are trapped in an abandoned house across the street. Do you want them dead or alive?" Ivan,"Alive if possible, dead if necessary."

Just as the Russians were getting ready to take the pair out, Lieutenant Sunan and his HUMVEE'S come rumbling around the corner. The soldier manning the machine gun fires a burst over the maneuvering Russians a Bull Horn blared out an order,"Stop where you are or the next one is going to be deadly. Drop your weapons and back off I will not warn you a second time, drop your weapons and BACK OFF!"The Russians laid their weapons on the ground and with hands up climbed into their vehicles slowly driving away.The Lieutenant aimed the Bull Horn at the house,"You two in the building come out with your hands up go prone so we can cuff you." The building door was opened slowly and Carl walked out laying his weapon on the sidewalk.CIA Agents,"Turn around while we cuff you." With the cuffs in place they steered Carl to the SUV,"Get in the back and keep quiet, we have to arrest your soul mate Henry, we've been looking to take you two down for years.You two will be in jail forever."

Chapter Forty

Marjorie orders Johnson,"When you arrest Henry separate him from Carl, make sure they are in different HUMVEE'S I don't want those two talking."

The Agents slowly entered the building with weapons drawn. "Henry come out with your hands up, we don't have time for this, Henry come out I won't ask again you mess with me and I will pop you." Agent,"Johnson, the place is empty, where in the hell is he?" Johnson,"You have to be kidding right."

"No sir!"

Carl sat looking out of the SUVs windows, heard that Henry has escaped, Johnson peers in at Carl,"Your buddy has left you to take the rap, where is he?" Carl smirked,"Henry who? have no idea who you are talking about."

"Look smart ass don't give me that bullshit. You'll be humming another tune when I water board your ugly butt." "AW,Johnson don't get your balls all twisted Henry just went to take a long pee" Carl answers laughing.

Marjorie walks to the SUV,"Lets go Johnson stop screwing with this perp get out there see if you can find Henry.

Lieutenant Sunan wants us out of this neighborhood before the sun goes down, the natives are restless."

While the CIA was arresting Carl,Henry was checking the rear of the building looking for a way out. As he ran his hand slowly along the rear wall he felt a draft,"Might be a way out." Took out his knife, he ran it down the seam and "POP" a hidden door opened. Henry stuck his head out of the door looking left and right, thinking,"ALL CLEAR! Carl will keep them busy while I get away." There was an old pink drape laying on the floor, he reached down digging a handful of dirt out of the bare floor pissed in it washed the dirt in a stinking rain puddle. Covered his face and hands to darken his skin, draped the pink curtain over his head and wrapped it around his body like a monks robe, picked up a crooked stick for a cane and stepped out of the building humming and repeating a MANTRA.

The Thai Soldiers checked the back of the building, Lieutenant Sunan,"Find anything around the back of the shack." Soldier,"Only person we saw was an old Monk hobbling down the street singing a MANTRA over and over." Lieutenant,"Did you question the Monk." Soldier,"We didn't get too close he stunk pretty bad, so we kind of kept our distance",the trooper held his nose. Lieutenant Sunan,"Alright, alright wrap it up for tonight we have to move. I want a HUMVEE at the head of the column and the other to follow in the rear." Sergeant,"Yes sir it is done,"Lieutenant Sunan,"Keep a sharp look out, I don't want any American's killed,"DO YOU UNDERSTAND?" Sergeant,"Yes Lieutenant we understand." Lieutenant,"Good" he walked off opened the door to his vehicle and sat in the passenger seat, "Don't look at me drive,"It was dark when the convoy arrived at the Embassy. Marjorie,"Pull the SUV around the rear of the Embassy then take our prisoner to a holding cell I will be there as soon as possible." Morrison is waiting inside when they brought Carl in,"Clean him up and put him in an orange jump suit." Carl,"Why don't you"FEDS" go screw I'm not telling you anything."Morrison punches Carl in the solar plexus, he doubles over falling to his knees and starts to puke." Morrison hollers,"JESUS, you asshole there is vomit on my shoes." Carl is laughing and vomiting at the sam time, Morrison you haven't changed you'r still a dumb flatfoot" Morrison raises his fist to punch Carl." Marjorie,"STOP NOW" enough of this. You two clean him up and put him in a cell."

Marjorie looks at Morrison,"Don't touch him again, if you do I will file charges against you, do you understand Agent Morrison?"

"Sorry, Marjorie, I couldn't help myself that creep is a murderer and a white slaver." Marjorie,"We need him in one alive so we can put him on trial in DC" Marjorie answers.

Chapter Forty One

"Captain there's a sad looking Monk looking for a boat ride to Myanmar.I told him this fishing boat didn't have any room" the crewman said holding his nose.

Captain,"Monks are holy men they worship Buddha and I am a devout Buddhist. Go tell him we have room. I will take him wherever he wishes." the crewman walks to the edge of the boat signaling to the Monk,"Come on the Captain said he will take you where ever you wish." Monk,"Thank you my son our Lord Buddha thanks you and blesses you."

Crewman,"OK, just step aboard so I can cast off."

The Monk stepped aboard, placed the blanket the crewman gave him on the deck and laid down. The rhythmic rocking of the boat lulled the Monk into a deep sleep something he had not had for a long, long time.

Ivan's phone kept ringing, he was thinking," that General Hong is like a frigging bull dog. He wants to know whether I took out Carl and Henry I don't want to listen to him rant and rave." The phone continued to ring in frustration Ivan answers,"WHAT!do you want General?" Hong,"Did you earn the money or not? What is this I hear that Carl has been arrested by the CIA and Henry is missing, shit Ivan you owe me half million dollars." Ivan looks at the phone not believing what he just heard.

At the Embassy Marjorie Swift is making preparations to have Carl transported to the States when there is a call from the Chinese Embassy in Bangkok. "Marjorie you have a call." Marjorie,"Who now?" Agent,"It's the Ambassador from the Chinese Embassy." Marjorie,"What in the hell does he want?" "They claim Carl has broken Chinese laws and have the right to prosecute him in China, he demands we turn him over immediately." Marjorie,"OH LORD, I see a real circus happening who in the hell put the information on the street that Carl has been arrested?" Agent,"I would link the info to the Russians.Besides them I don't have a clue, but the Chinese Ambassador is adamant" Marjorie,"Put him on the phone and call Ambassador Gibbs let him know what is going on."

"Hello Ambassador how are you today?" she pulled the phone away from her ear as the Chinese Ambassador started screaming into the phone. Marjorie let him rant till he ran out of breath,"Ambassador, Carl is a US citizen and wanted for murdering six women in the United States, plus miscellaneous other crimes. We have jurisdiction and if I remember correctly you'r country refused to sign an extradition treaty with the US."

Chinese Ambassador,"That thief has bilked the Chinese people out of millions of dollars, we need to question him so we can recoup the lost money." Marjorie listens patiently before answering, "When we have convicted the prisoner and he has served his sentence, only then will you be able to question him, if my government allows it, I recommend you file a complaint with the State Department."Marjorie hung up.

She reaches down and opens her desk drawer pulls out her bottle of Bourbon and two pills.Pours herself a full glass of the nectar, pops the pills washing them down with the bourbon,"OH GOD! I needed that!" Her Aide walks in,"Boss you are not going to believe this, but the Russian Ambassador is on the phone he wants us to turn Carl over to them, claims Carl illegally stole weapons and sold them to Insurgents hostile to their government."

Marjorie,"Do me a favor inform the Russian Ambassador that he should put his complaint in writing and the American Ambassador will review it." Aide,"Yes Ma'am sounds perfect." "Good just do it."

She poured herself another drink, the pills had just begun to calm her down she didn't need this bullshit all it did was get her blood pressure up. There was a knock on her door. "Come in." Morrison walks in with a smirk on his face breaks down laughing,"You wanted to be the Bureau Chief, I just received info that the Cambodian Government wants to sue Carl for corruption of their citizens, the Vietnamese for drug smuggling and Laos for gun running and corrupting the people of a sovereign nation." Morrison is laughing so hard tears are running down his cheeks,"AND... AND we haven't heard from Myanmar and India yet." Marjorie has to laugh,"Who, in the hell haven't they pissed off, God I need that vacation to France real, real bad before I have a nervous breakdown.

Morrison do me a favor and put Carl on the next plane out of Thailand before there are protestors outside of the Embassy gates" Marjorie orders. Morrison,"He will be gone by morning you need to go on vacation ASAP with your daughter, you both need some bonding time."

"Carl could hear the guard walking toward his cell,"I wonder what they want now?" Guard,"Let's go Carl" one guard placed a hood over his head guided him out of the cell.

Prison Guard,"Just walk and keep quiet, we're moving you to a more secure prison." Carl was escorted to a Cargo Plane, and manacled to the wall. As the the plane taxied for take off, he wondered,"Where in the hell are they taking me."

Marjorie and her daughter took off for France later that night.